WARNING

WELCOME TO THE **TRIGGER WARNING** PAGE, YOU DIRTY-MINDED LITTLE FREAKS. IF YOU ARE ANYTHING LIKE US AND ENJOY THE THOUGHT OF BEING RAILED BY AN ANGEL...OR EVEN A DEMON, PLEASE DISREGARD THIS PAGE AND CARRY ON WITH YOUR NASTY LITTLE FANTASY.

WHAT LIES BETWEEN MAY CONTAIN TRIGGERS FOR SOME.

TRIGGER WARNINGS INCLUDE BUT ARE NOT LIMITED TO:
GRAPHIC VIOLENCE, EXPLICIT LANGUAGE, MULTIPLE PARTNERS, BREATH PLAY, MASKS, ALCOHOL USE, SEXUAL CONTENT, FANTASY MIND CONTROL, BLOOD PLAY

WHAT LIES BETWEEN

Content Notice

This book contains **graphic violence** and **sexual content**. It is not intended for anyone under the age of legal adulthood. All characters depicted herein are adults. This book is not to be used as a resource for sexual education or as an informational guide to sex or BDSM. **The activities and scenes are not meant to depict realistic expectations of BDSM or fetish-related activities......but you can always dream.**
Reader's discretion is strongly advised.

This book is a work of fiction. Names, characters, places, and incidents either are a product of the author's imagination or are used fictitiously.

WHAT LIES BETWEEN

Playlist

A CURATED LIST OF SONGS FROM THE AUTHORS TO HELP IMMERSE YOURSELF IN THE SCENE. ASTERISKS (***) ARE PLACED NEXT TO THE COINCIDING SCENE

CHAPTER 1 - HEAVY IS THE CROWN BY: MIKE SHINODA & EMILY ARMSTRONG

CHAPTER 24 - SKIN AND BONES BY: DAVID KUSHNER

CHAPTER 55 - DIRTY THOUGHTS BY: CHLOE ADAMS

CHAPTER 65 - THE LINE BY: TWENTY ONE PILOTS

CHAPTER 69 - I FEEL LIKE A GOD BY: DEATHBYROMY

CHAPTER 75 - RUNAWAY BY: AURORA

CHAPTER 89 - MY BLOOD BY: ELLIE GOULDING

WHAT LIES BETWEEN

WHAT LIES BETWEEN

WRITTEN BY AUTHORS: C.N. PETTIT & T.D. FINDLEY

DEDICATIONS:

TO MY HUSBAND AND DAUGHTERS, WHO PUT UP WITH ME SITTING BEHIND A COMPUTER SCREEN IN MY FREE TIME, AND TO YOUR CONTRIBUTIONS WHEN MY MIND WAS STUCK.
TO CATHERINE (YOU KNOW WHO YOU ARE), WITHOUT YOUR IMAGINATION, FOCUS, AND DRIVE, THIS WOULD STILL BE A PASSING THOUGHT. -T.D. FINDLEY

TO MY BROTHER, MAY YOU LIVE FOREVER HERE.
-C.N. PETTIT

GUIDE TO WHAT LIES BETWEEN
ARCANE: FACTIONS OF MAGIC

FIRE- RULING GOD: VULCAN. FACTION COLOR: RED. CONTROL/MANIPULATION OF FIRE

WATER- RULING GOD: NEPTUNE. FACTION COLOR: BLUE. CONTROL/MANIPULATION OF WATER

EARTH- RULING GOD: GAIA. FACTION COLOR: GREEN. CONTROL/MANIPULATION OF EARTH

AIR- RULING GOD: SHU. FACTION COLOR: WHITE. CONTROL/MANIPULATION OF AIR

NECROMANCY- RULING GOD: CATO. FACTION COLOR: PURPLE. ABILITY TO CONTROL THE DEAD, RESURRECTION, SUMMON SPIRITS, AND COMMUNE WITH THE AFTERLIFE

HEALING- RULING GOD: APOLLO. FACTION COLOR: YELLOW. ABILITY TO HEAL INJURIES, ILLNESSES, AND MENTAL ISSUES

TIME- RULING GOD: CRONOS. FACTION COLORS: SILVER. CONTROL/MANIPULATION OF TIME, SEE PAST OCCURRENCES, AND PROPHESIZE THE FUTURE

CHAOS- RULING GOD: LOKI. FACTION COLOR: BLACK. ABILITY TO MANIPULATE A BEING'S MIND AND CREATE ILLUSIONS

DEFINITIONS:

HELLION-/HEL-YUN/ DEMON LIKE BEING

ELYSIAN-/UH-LIS-EE-AN/ ANGELIC BEING

NEPHILIM-/NEF-I-LIM/ MIXED BLOOD BEING OF EITHER HELLION/MORTAL OR ANGEL/MORTAL

CHIMERA-/KY-MER-UH/ A MIXED BLOOD BEING OF AN ANIMAL AND A MORTAL. FOR EXAMPLE, WIXEN-FOX/MORTAL HYBRID, LYNX- CAT/MORTAL HYBRID, ARCHONS- REPTILE/MORTAL, CERVITAUR-DEER/MORTAL HYBRID

ELEMENTAL SPRITE- SMALL FAIRY-LIKE BEINGS WITH EARTH, AIR, FIRE, AND WATER MAGIC

WINDEMERE-/WIND-UH-MEER/ WORLD OF THE LIVING. CAPITAL: SWINDON

ELYSIA-/UH-LIS-EE-UH/CELESTIAL LAND

HELHEIM-/HELL-HYME/UNDERWORLD

WHAT LIES BETWEEN

WHAT LIES BETWEEN

CHAPTER 1

EDIN

Autumn in Windemere is breathtaking. The dense pink, green, and yellow trees cover the high sprawling mountains, making a beautiful backdrop for the opulent Swindon Castle which sits at the foothills of the largest mountain in the realm. The sunset turns the sky into a colorful mix of orange and purple as I walk through the tall archway doors to the grand hall. Autumn florals adorn

every candle-lit sconce, leading me to the gathering.
Walking down the long hallway, I take in the high vaulted
ceilings with large, detailed banners hung in honor of each
arcane. Massive marble carvings of the gods stand at each
flag. I walk under the banners and stop to pay respect to
each of the gods. *Vulcan, God of Fire,* I nod my head and
continue. *Neptune, God of Water. Gaia, Goddess of the
Earth. Shu, God of Air. Cato, God of Death and Purgatory.*
I smile as I step in front of the next statue. *Apollo, God of
Healing.* I stand a moment longer, then move to the next.
Cronos, God of Time. My hands begin to shake as I step in
front of the last statue. *Loki, God of Chaos.* Chaos magic is
a rare and powerful arcane, with the ability to manipulate
one's mind. I take a deep breath, holding my shoulders
back and chin up, even though I feel completely out of my
element.

WHAT LIES BETWEEN

Tonight is the annual Enlightenment; the day most have waited their entire lives for. It is the moment a god grants a being with power, and they find their place in the realm. Eager conversations echo through the doors as I reach the end of the hall. The foyer finally spills into the ceremony room, and I can almost feel the vibrations of excitement. So many masked onlookers have me feeling exposed as I walk past with my face uncovered. Only the enlightened can wear the intricate mask that honors the god or goddess from whom they have received their power, and tonight it is finally my turn. My entire lineage has been given healing magic from the god Apollo, and in a matter of minutes, King Thayer will be bestowing me with that same power. Nonetheless, anxious anticipation creeps slowly through my body. It is said that when receiving your power it can be painful, yet others describe it as exhilarating. I have never been afraid of pain, but the daunting anticipation weighs heavily on my mind, making my steps slow and my breathing shallow.

Pulling myself from nervous thoughts, I spot Blythe sauntering up, wearing a gorgeous violet corset dress with black lace filigree along the neckline and sleeves. The plunge of her neckline and cinched waist leave little to the imagination. Her mask covers most of her face, except for her thick red lips and dainty chin. Her mask is beautifully detailed, depicting the face of Gaia. We have been friends since we were small and have become inseparable. "You did an amazing job, the flowers here are beautiful," I say, rubbing my arm anxiously.

"Thank you, I grew them myself," Blythe jokes, as her eyes track my hand movements. Taking me by the hand

and kissing my cheeks she says, "Seriously though, I know you are nervous, and I don't blame you, but everything will be just fine." She pulls me in tightly, continuing, "Just think, when you are granted your power, the jolt of magic may just give you a tingly sensation in your lady bits! Gods know you need to get laid," she giggles, and her fox ears perk up, "Anywho, wish me luck, I'm off to find a beautiful busty lady with loose morals to hide in an alcove with." She gives me a sly smile, twirling her short auburn curls as she sets off to watch the ceremony from the crowd. Blythe has always been the lighthearted ray of sunshine that I need when I am anxious. I am so thankful for her presence tonight. Off to the right of the dais, I see my mother and father eagerly anticipating tonight's festivities, both dressed in their finest and wearing golden masks adorned with the rays of the sun, representing Apollo and his healing magic. I nod to them both and turn to get into position.

***

King Thayer's booming voice calls me up to the dais. Ignoring my racing heart, I walk with an air of confidence to the center. Kneeling on the Enlightening Stone, the King lays both hands on my shoulders, giving me a squeeze of reassurance before setting the altar ablaze. "Edin of Blackburn," he announces. A thick purple fog crawls up the edges of the stone and swirls around me, engulfing my body in a suffocating cloud. "You have been granted the power of necromancy!" *Wait? What?* Time feels as though it stands still. I turn my head to the side, scanning the crowd, and I meet my mother's gaze. There is a look of confusion in her eyes, but she mouths "It's okay," with a smile. Suddenly time rushes back into focus as I am taken over by shock waves that rip through my body. Flashes of bright light blind me, and my lungs burn with each shallow breath. Clawing at my throat, I gasp for air. A stifling heat envelopes my body as sweat forms a sheen over my skin. After what seems like a lifetime, the feeling subsides, and the fog begins to dissipate. My breaths come easier and the heat fades leaving me shaking on the dais. Slowly sitting up and sliding myself off the dais, I attempt to collect myself.

"How can this be?" I ask under my breath, still in shock. Just as I begin to relax, my gut clenches. A second flash of light hits my chest so hard it reverberates throughout my ribcage, like an echo of pain, sending me back onto my knees. Looking down, a dark image begins to appear along my sternum of a set of wings that fan out from each side of a sword, and a set of scales hang from its hilt.

An ethereal voice sounds from above, and the image of Cato, God of Purgatory, appears before us: "The scales of judgment adorn the chest of the new Goddess of Purgatory, in semblance of her destiny. The power to open the veil between Elysia and Helheim will now be passed to you, Edin of Blackburn. You alone will decide the fate of all souls who cross over into your realm. Be true and sure in your decision, their fate is in your hands." Cato bows his head and takes his leave with only a mist remaining in his place. My mind reels.

"How have I been given a goddess title?" I ask myself, staring down at the tile. I pull my shaking body up from the floor and stumble down the stairs.

Necromancy? Goddess of Purgatory? I am meant to be a healer.

Peering through the sea of people, I look for Blythe, hoping she is not already two fingers deep in a lady. To my surprise, I spot her across the room heading toward me, with a bottle of wine and two glasses in hand. "I thought you could use some liquid courage! I swiped this from the royal kitchen, it's winter wine!" Blythe says with a giggle as she pours me a glass. In true Wixen fashion, only Blythe could get away with thieving from Swindon Castle's kitchen. Winter wine is brewed much stronger to help get a being through the rough winters here in Windemere.

"What in all of Helheim just happened, Blythe?"

Her smile fades, "Honestly, I don't know. A god title hasn't been bestowed since The War of Realms."

"And necromancy?" I huff.

"Again, I don't know, Love. I'm just as stunned as you are," she says, laying her hand on my cheek, "But it seems you've caught someone's eye." Blythe nods her head towards the gentleman making his way through the crowd.

"Shit," I groan, downing my glass and raising it to Blythe for a second pour.

"Go and have some fun, Love. Gods know you need it," she laughs, sending me off with a pat on my ass.

CHAPTER 2

OSIRIS

Straightening my mask as I make my way across the crowded dance floor, I spot Edin in the corner, downing an entire glass of wine. I assume she must need to calm her nerves after being granted the new title. Undoubtedly, she was not expecting such a grand appointment. She is stunning in her emerald green dress, hugging every curve so effortlessly. Even without the title, she *is* truly a goddess. The stark contrast of her milky white skin to her ebony hair is exquisite, with the peculiar silver streak that frames her face.

"Edin of Blackburn," I greet her, bowing low, "General Osiris, leader of the Elysian Army. I thought I would take this opportunity to introduce myself, as I will

21

be assisting you in the guidance of souls to Elysia until your training is complete."

The faintest flicker of shock in her eyes is immediately hidden away as she straightens her shoulders. "I appreciate your introduction and will be looking forward to your accompaniment in Purgatory," she curtsies.

Edin may only be around five foot two, but the confidence in her tone and posture is substantial, stirring something within me.

"May I have this dance?" I ask, holding out my hand. She lays her hand in mine, sending a shock through me, as we step onto the dance floor.

Her steps perfectly match mine as I spin her around, the scent of vanilla and clove fills the air. "I feel

congratulations are in order," I say, dipping her low to the
ground before bringing her close to my chest.

Edin lays her hand on my chest, and the electricity
builds where our bodies connect. "It was very unexpected,
but thank you. How often will you be making your
appearance, if I may ask?" she questions.

"You will be seeing quite a lot of me until you are
able to open the veil yourself. Death waits for no one," I
give her a light-hearted laugh, as I remove my mask and
hook it to my belt.

CHAPTER 3

EDIN

Dear gods, Osiris is beautiful, but of course he is, he is Elysian. He must be at least six foot four with the way he towers over me. His long, red, wavy hair and cropped beard seem brighter against his dark eyes. The deep grey color of his eyes reminds me of the sky just before a great thunderstorm, matching the gray in the feathers of his wings that hang over his formidable frame...And his mask, he wields the power of chaos magic.

The music slows down to a simple beat, giving Osiris the opportunity to ask, "You are from Blackburn, correct?"

"Yes, it is in the northern bounds of Windemere. Are you familiar?"

"Unfortunately, no. I dream of traveling the realms, but my duty keeps me quite busy," he sullenly replies.

I smile up at him, "Traveling is also a dream of mine." A waiter slides past us, and I reach for a glass of sparkling ale as Osiris slowly spins me.

"Would you like to step out onto the balcony?" he nods his head towards the wall of crystal-paned doors.

I smile, "Some fresh air would be nice."

He takes my hand, guiding me through the crowd. I swipe one more glass of ale before stepping out into the cool autumn air. Osiris leans over the balcony, taking in the view, "It is beautiful here."

I laugh, "I am sure it is nothing compared to Elysia."

He chuckles, "I am sure you will be able to see it for yourself soon."

I look out over the mountainscape, finishing the last of my ale in an attempt to drown my nerves. Turning back around, I watch through the window as the candles begin to dim.

Osiris bumps my shoulder, grinning, "This is when the real party starts."

"What do you mean?" I raise an eyebrow.

"All of the higher-ups leave and they start playing some decent music. Come on," he says, grabbing my hand and pulling me inside.

The entire atmosphere of the room has shifted. What was once a regal gathering is now a roaring celebration. Half the candles have been blown out, and the others have colorful shades set on them, casting hues of color across the grand ceiling. The music is fast-paced and much louder. The masked attendees are no longer dancing at arm's length, moving their bodies as one to the beat of the music.

"Would you like to join the crowd?" Osiris chuckles, raising an eyebrow at me. Grabbing yet another glass of ale, I toss it back as quickly as possible.

"Yes," I giggle, taking his outstretched hand.

I can not tell if it is the winter wine or Osiris' heavenly scent of teakwood and sea salt that is making my head spin. I refuse to care tonight, my entire world has been turned on its head, but that will be a problem for tomorrow. Throwing all my morals aside, I push my back against his broad chest, grinding my hips. I take just a moment to scan the crowd, spotting Blythe hand in hand with a beautiful lady, as they make their way towards the exit.

Pulling me back to his gaze, Osiris asks, "You said your enlightenment was unexpected, did you have your heart set elsewhere?"

Stumbling on the verge of drunkenness while attempting to explain my lineage sounds like a feat I am ill-prepared for. How does one explain that their entire ancestry had only ever been gifted with the power of healing, a rare oddity for sure. Thankfully, before I can respond, Osiris sends me spinning around, and I am in a new set of toned arms.

Looking up, I find a pair of bright sky-blue eyes behind a mask I have never seen before. The mask looks to honor two gods, Vulcan, the God of fire, and Neptune, the God of water, clashing beautifully straight down the middle. I have never met anyone blessed by two gods, but the man before me could be a god himself, standing at what looked to be six foot six, if not more. He leans me low into a dip and meets my eyes with a stony gaze. My heart races and my thighs clench. I assume he will introduce himself, but he says nothing. He pulls me back up, and I steady myself for another spin. I spin around, muttering under my breath, "What in Hera's sweet name was that?" I am met again with the familiar strong arms of Osiris, but not without the hands of the masked man behind me on my hips. I lay both my hands on Osiris' chest and press my ass against my newfound acquaintance, truly throwing my morals to the wind. Looking up at Osiris, I attempt to give him my best *kiss me* eyes. I feel the snaking hand of the masked man run up my backside and around my throat, pushing my head back against his hard chest.

Osiris takes my hint and growls, "Is this what you want, Little Hellion?" as our lips meet. The spark from our lips almost matches the burning urge swirling in my core. Gods, I really must be drunk if the thought of two men at once sounds as good as they currently feel pressed up against both sides of my body. I assume from the roaming hand of the masked man making his way from my throat to my inner thigh, he agrees. The hungry look in Osiris' eyes is also a good indication. Both men take a quick glance at each other for confirmation before they tug me off the dance floor and down a candle-lit hallway.

Osiris intertwines his fingers with mine, "Are you sure you want this, Edin?" he asks, rubbing his thumb against the back of my hand.

"Yes," I nod, looking at both men.

The masked man chuckles, "As you wish," grabbing a handful of my hair and leading me into the first unlocked set of doors.

I am scrambling for words at the sight of the stately den before me. Thousands of books line the walls with tufted leather couches that sit across from each other. An onyx fireplace stands at the focal point of the room, and the masked man lights it with nothing more than a flick of his wrist. Barely able to take in the entirety of the room,

Osiris takes a seat, pulling me onto his lap, facing away from him. He quickly unlaces my dress in the process.

The masked man takes a moment to undo his belt and wraps it around my throat in a leash-like fashion. He pulls me forward, to the end of Osiris's thighs, and devours my mouth as I unbutton his trousers, pulling his cock out. I can feel Osiris sliding his trousers down behind me.

The masked man growls, "If you really want it, Miss Goddess of Purgatory, then sit yourself down on General Osiris," sending me over the edge.

Absolutely dripping, while also wanting to show this man just who he is speaking to, I slam down on Osiris's long length, ignoring the burning stretch. I reach for the masked man, running my hand down his shaft, counting the barbells out loud, "One, two, three, four, five, six," I snicker, licking my lips. I look up at him to meet his gaze, while I continue slowly circling my hips.

Osiris grabs me by the waist, obviously wanting to pick up the pace, hitting the bundle of nerves deep inside me. My moan is abruptly cut off by the masked man taking the open opportunity, sliding his cock into my mouth, hitting the back of my throat. I have not been this brutally fucked since the Samhain Festival two hundred years ago. *Blythe was right, I did need this*. Tension builds deep in my pussy as Osiris pounds into me. I tug on the masked man's balls as I hollow my cheeks, bringing him as far down my throat as possible. All the candles in the room suddenly go out. I am left with only the bright lights exploding behind my eyelids, as I ride out the waves of pleasure while my new masked acquaintance spills onto my freshly marked chest and Osiris follows suit. The rush of my orgasm drains the last of my energy, leaving me in a drunken stupor. Suddenly, I am fighting to even keep my eyes open as I am lifted onto the leather couch, cleaned, and covered with a blanket. I faintly hear "Good girl," before completely dozing off.

CHAPTER 4

EDIN

Three Days Prior…

I wake up to a banging at my window. I see a set of furry fox ears and hands hanging on for life from my windowsill. "Blythe?" I yawn, crawling out of bed.

Perpetually an early riser, my best friend is always ready to stir up mischief. "How in Hera's name can you be asleep when we only have three days to prepare for your enlightening?" she squeals, as I hoist her through the window. "You have to look absolutely beddable."

Rolling my eyes, "Elegant," I correct her. "I am not dressing myself for the male gaze, Blythe."

She throws herself down on my bed, whining, "You haven't been screwed in months. No wonder you're so testy. You need to get laid."

Blythe lies on my bed lazily, chattering on about what my dress should look like. "I think we need to look for a severely low-cut dress, you know, to really show off your assets!" she teases, pushing her own breasts up. I am not surprised in the least, I have always been the more guarded one.

"My tits are staying firmly in my bodice, thank you," I huff, pulling on my pants and tunic.

"Your body is so sexy, but no one would know with the way *you* dress." Blythe whines as we head to the foyer to tell my parents that we are leaving for the city.

WHAT LIES BETWEEN

I find them out in the gardens, tending to their herbs. My parents inherited our ancestors' local apothecary. Along with magic, they use herbs to make potions and salves as healing aids for emergencies and ailments. My mother, Odessa, could have been mistaken for having earth magic, with her green thumb. The garden is always so lush and bountiful. I could be her twin with her pointed ears and short black horns, except for my ebony hair that came from my father, Ronan. My mother has the most beautiful long silver hair that is almost opalescent. I am thankful to at least have a streak of it. My siblings did not receive as many Nephilim traits, looking more like our father, who is mortal.

I give my mother a kiss on the cheek before waving goodbye, as Blythe and I set off on our journey. We must travel to the center of Swindon, several villages away from Blackburn, my home since my birth. Windemere is home to many walks of life, from the chimera, like Blythe, who carry both mortal and animal DNA. Windemere is also home to Elysians, Hellions, Centaurs, and Sprites. Sprites alone have their own factions, each one holding an elemental from fire, earth, wind, to water. At almost mid-morning, we pass the quaint river cottages at the base of the mountains, home to the earth sprites. I give Blythe a nudge to keep her voice low. Earth sprites are the most adorable little brown creatures with pointy ears, branches protruding from their skulls that almost look like antlers and root-like skin that grows flowers and vines. However, they can be very mischievous. Earth sprites are known for starting fights with anyone who dares to disturb their rest, even each other. We keep our steps quiet and voices below a whisper to not disrupt the village.

We thankfully leave the earth sprite village, and are back to walking the dirt path through the forest. Another hour passes as the outskirts of Kayliss comes into view. Kayliss is a merchant town right outside Swindon. We pull our totes close to our chest as we walk over the village bridge into town. Kayliss is wonderful for shopping for trinkets and enchanted items but is also known for pick-pocketers and swindlers. I pull my cloak over my head and Blythe takes me by the hand, pulling me through the bustling crowd.

"Do you not want to say hello to some old friends?" I giggle, questioning Blythe.

She rolls her eyes at me, "I would prefer not."

Kayliss used to be Blythe's stomping ground. She was a master con artist, taking advantage of her fox-like characteristics. We quickly make our way through the village, avoiding any on-lookers, and out of the village gates.

Back into the cover of the tree, Blythe lets out a deep breath, huffing, "Thank the Gods."

I giggle, "You know if you would just pay your dues back in Kayliss, everything would be fine."

"I won the coins fair and square, not my fault that the fire sprite was too slow," Blythe grumbles.

"Whatever you say, Blythe," I continue laughing, rolling my eyes back at her.

CHAPTER 5

EDIN

Finally, we reach the city limits of Swindon, the capital city of Windemere. The cobblestone streets are lined with the moss-covered buildings of storefronts and eateries. All the structures are adorned with intricate designs built by the ancient inhabitants many years ago. We reach Azara's Boutique intending to find the perfect gown for the Enlightenment, *or* if Blythe has her way, show all of Windemere my cleavage. This shop has always been the best in the city, as Azara has impeccable taste and an eye for beauty. As soon as we walk through the doors Blythe is immediately on a rampage, scouring through the dresses for one that has as little fabric as possible.

Rolling my eyes at Blythe, I greet Azura warmly, "Hello, Azura, so nice to see you again."

"Oh, hello ladies, here to find gowns for the ceremony?" She motions me toward the back of the store. "I just got some new garments delivered yesterday. I'm sure there is something here befitting our honoree."

I start to scan the room, but almost immediately spot a luminescent green gown with golden inlay that matches my eyes perfectly.

"Here, try these on!" Blythe interrupts, laying out a menagerie of dresses that would barely cover my front or backside.

Ignoring her, I take the green dress to the fitting area to try it on. I slip into the luxurious fabric and it fits like a glove. I have always been thankful for my toned figure. Stepping out, I start to ask, "How do I-", but before the words can leave my mouth, Blythe's excitement overtakes her.

"You are so stunning! I have dreamt of this day since we were little. I'm so glad to be a part of your big day, even if you won't entertain my idea of dazzling the audience with your busty chest," she laughs, pulling me in for a hug.

I have always loved Blythe, not in the way she loves the ladies, but in a way that I could not imagine my life without her. Blythe, in true fashion, finds a gown with an under-bust corset and just enough material to barely cover her chest. We find shoes and jewelry to match our gowns and pay Azura before we start to make our way back to our small village of Blackburn.

WHAT LIES BETWEEN

Windemere is such a vast realm. I wonder, as we walk, where I would be placed following the ceremony. Most healers were placed in Swindon to tend to the soldiers, but some were lucky enough, like my parents, to stay in their home village. I know I will be an exceptional healer after many years of assisting my parents. Fortunately, our realm has been at peace for thousands of years with Elysia and Helheim, so it is possible I will not be needed as a healer to the kingdom. As much as I would adore working side by side with my parents, seeing more of Windemere has always been a dream of mine. I have been told on the southern shores the climate is much warmer, with miles of sand that kisses the great sea. While on the eastern border, there are trees that stand at a height that matches the clouds, clustered so close it blocks out the light in areas. Blackburn is set on the northern bounds, with a dramatic mountain range, evergreen forest, and jagged rocky coastlines. It is the most beautiful landscape in the realm, but I may be biased.

CHAPTER 6

BLYTHE

We walk side by side, our arms brushing as we make our way down the path. "Are you ready for the Enlightenment, Love?" I ask.

"I think so, I am honestly kind of nervous," Edin shrugs.

"What is there to be nervous about? You will receive your healing magic and then officially join your family's apothecary."

"But what if I don't, Blythe?"

"Seriously, Edin, it's pretty much a myth for an entire lineage to only be given one power. You really think you will be an entirely different oddity?" I rub Edin's shoulder and say, "You will be just fine, Love."

She intertwines her fingers in mine, "Thank you, what would I ever do without you?" Edin smiles at me.

"You will never have to find out," I assure her, squeezing her hand. The sun begins to set, casting swirls of pink and orange across the sky. We walk in silence taking in the view. "You know…there will be loads of fine-ass gentlemen at the ceremony," I laugh, bumping Edin's shoulder.

"I am sure there will be," she responds un-entertained.

"Fine-ass gentlemen from all three realms," I pry again, wiggling my eyebrows.

"You do not even like men, Blythe," she laughs.

"This is true but, it doesn't mean I don't enjoy looking. Gods! Those Elysian men, they look like walking bronze statues!"

Edin rolls her eyes, "Yes, well, they *are* angelic beings."

"And don't get me started on the Hellions, dark horned and mysterious, makes me question things."

"I swear you are always horny, Blythe," she giggles.

The mossy stone walls of Blackburn finally come into view. We watch as the town's fire sprite slowly sets hanging lanterns alight throughout the village.

CHAPTER 7

EDIN

Walking down the rocky path through Blackburn, I give Blythe a kiss on the cheek before heading for my family home. My home is not grand, a modest two-story stone cottage my great-great-grandfather built himself. The small details of the stained glass windows, the ones my grandmother made by hand, and the wooden flower pots lining each window below make it feel cozy. Blythe made sure when she received her earth magic last year that the pots were full of blooming flowers year round. Blackburn is a small town and I would be happy to start lending my healing hands here, once the Enlightenment is over. Pushing through the old wooden door as quietly as possible so as to not wake my siblings, I spot my mother sitting by the fire.

"Come sit, sweet girl, tell me all about your adventure," she says, reaching her hand out to me.

I take her hand and squeeze in next to her, laying my head on her shoulder. My mother is my comfort, a guiding light, and a familiar shoulder I have cried on many times. She always knows exactly what to say, giving the best advice. I tell her about our trip to the city and how Blythe picked every low-cut, revealing gown she could find for me to try on.

"Is there anything else you need for the Enlightenment?" she asks.

"No, I am well prepared," I say, picking at my fingers.

She lays her hand over mine, "What is troubling you, my girl?"

"Just nerves," I say, avoiding her stare.

"You have nothing to worry about," she warmly responds, tucking my hair behind my pointed ear. I begin to argue, but she stops me, laying a palm on each of my cheeks, "You are a beautiful, intelligent, and ambitious woman, and I am so proud of the young lady that you have become. I know that you will do well in all of your endeavors. Just don't lose sight of your personal goals while you head out to conquer the world."

"Thank you mother," I smile, embracing her, pushing all my nerves aside.

"You need to rest, lots to do before the ceremony. Goodnight my sweet girl," she says, kissing my forehead.

I blow out the candles, making my way up the stairs before quietly closing the door to my bedroom, which I share with my sisters. I refuse to let my nerves get to me, repeating my mother's words of wisdom as I doze off.

Rubbing my eyes I am awakened by Della, the youngest in the family, jumping on the bed. "Tomorrow is the day!" she squeals, landing at the foot. "Oh, sister! How excited are you?" she asks, crawling on top of me.

"I am very excited, Little Love, but it will just be another day. You know I will come back home afterwards, to start actually helping in the apothecary." I had been tasked with jarring all of our mother's salves and tonics, it would be nice to have a bit of a change.

"But sister, what if you are not blessed with healing? What if you are granted time or an elemental magic?"

I playfully tussle her hair, "As unlikely as that is, I guess I could become a prophet, or maybe an ironsmith." Our family's lineage of healing could be traced back millennia, a rarity, but we have become quite proficient in it and have mountains of journals from our ancestors. "Come on, let's go help Mother with breakfast," I say, hoisting her off of me.

The smell of honey biscuits floats through the air as we descend the stairs. I find my mother in her usual morning spot, kneading fresh dough while my father is off opening the apothecary.

"Good morning, Mother." I smile, taking my place next to her to shape the dough into rounds. Mornings have always been my favorite time, all my siblings, besides Della, are out setting up shop while we prepare breakfast. The quiet house, small conversations, and the smell of warm honey butter make for the perfect start to one's day.

"Mother," Della chirps, "tell me about the Enlightenment."

"That is quite fitting for our day tomorrow, Della," Odessa says as she brushes honey across each steaming biscuit. "The Enlightenment is one of the most special days of each being's life. The gods watch over us from the time we are born into this world and carefully deliberate where we fit best into it, before deciding our magic. Once a soul has reached a thousand years old, a decision is made by the deity council. Then, a specific god will bless you with a sliver of their own arcane at the ceremony, trusting you to use it wisely and always for good."

"What if you don't?" Della questions.

"I suppose you will be dealt with by Cato."

"Cato?" Della asks.

"Oh yes, Cato, the most recent God of Purgatory, he awaits your demise to cast his judgment and decide your fate." Fear runs across Della's face. "Do not worry your little head though, you are as sweet as they come," Odessa says, grabbing Della's cheek. "Any plans for today, Edin?" she asks, patting the flour from her hands onto her apron.

"I plan to treat it as a normal day and help father out in the apothecary."

"How boring! Starting tomorrow you will be doing that for the rest of your life," Della laughs.

"Then it will be a normal day," I smirk.

The bang of the door swinging open cuts off our argument. "Is that Odessa's famous honey biscuits I smell?" Blythe asks, plopping down into a chair. "Good morning, Blythe. Set the table, will you dear?" my mother responds with a sweet smile. Blythe sets the table in record time and we finish our breakfast even quicker before heading to deliver biscuits to the apothecary.

CHAPTER 8

BLYTHE

"I swear, your mother makes the best honey biscuits in all of Windemere," I tell Edin, rubbing my stomach. "I could eat ten. She must enchant them."

"No enchantment," Edin giggles. "Just love, my mother says." Holding open the door to the apothecary, Edin carries in the usual basket stacked high with steaming biscuits for the rest of her siblings and father. "Good morning, father!" she yells towards the back, making her presence known.

"Good morning, my girl!" her father yells back, tripping through the swinging doors with scrolls tucked under each arm and a crate of pots and elixir decanters in his hands. "And good morning, Miss Blythe!"

"Good morning, Ronan, we have the usual for you!" I watch as all of Edin's siblings show up out of nowhere like she has summoned a small army. Being an only child, I have always been thankful for our friendship, and the kindness of her family. Moving to Blackburn with my parents at a young age from the southern border was terrifying enough, but to have no other siblings was the worst part. I was relieved to meet Edin within the first few days of moving and her family immediately treated me as their own.

CHAPTER 9

EDIN

My father is the kindest of souls, but quite a mess. Controlled chaos he would say. "Where can I help today?" I ask him.

"Well, I do have some orders to be packed," my father says, squinting his eyes at a list. "If only I could find my spectacles."

I carefully take his glasses from atop his head and place them on his nose with a giggle. "Better?"

"Ah, much! It looks like a couple pots of healing salve need to be packaged and delivered over to Astra, the water sprite," he chuckles, "The irony, seems she needs it for a burn."

I snort at his remark. It is quite clear I get my dark humor from him.

I hurriedly grab the needed supplies and begin preparing Astra's order. Blythe gives me a quick kiss on the cheek.

"I'll be back soon. I just need to make final adjustments on the florals for the Enlightenment," she yells over her shoulder as she walks out. My father steps up beside me and starts filling glass bottles with sagebrush tonics, a healing aid for on-the-go.

"Father?"

"Yes, my girl?"

"I know how we receive our power from the gods during the Enlightenment, but why are we granted them in the first place?" I ask.

"The War of Realms," he says, adjusting his glasses. "Two millenniums ago, before the arcane was obtained, the late King Sterling of Windemere gathered his army to assume control of all three realms. His militia was able to break the veil to Purgatory, giving him access to both Elysia and Helheim. Obviously, this act did not go over well with the people of the kingdom. They formed a rebellion and chaos broke out in all three lands. The war lasted for over ten years. The casualty rate was insurmountable, and so the rebels began to call out to the gods for aid. The gods heard their cries and descended to the realms to assist. Each god reigned down with their own form of terror, annihilating all who had disrupted the peace in our worlds. As a show of appreciation for our faith in the gods, they bestowed each being with a small amount of their own power."

I huff, "King Sterling sounds lovely," and roll my eyes sarcastically.

He continues, "That is why, each year for the Enlightenment, we don our masks as a remembrance of the ones we lost, a celebration of peace between our three realms, and in honor of the gods who did not forsake us."

I knew our magic was a gift from the gods, but I was not aware of all the bloodshed. "That is beautiful, in the darkest of ways," I say.

He pats me on the back, "But that's enough serious chatter for a year. I will finish packing up these orders, you run along. You will have all the time in the world to work in the apothecary after your ceremony."

I load Astra's order into the crate and gather my things. "Thank you, father. I will deliver this on my way home," I say, hoisting up the large crate and walking out.

CHAPTER 10

EDIN

I make my way down the cobblestone path, coming up on Astra's cottage. The tiny home is beautiful. It hangs over the edge of the river, with stacked grey stones, and a small waterfall that runs down the side. I walk over the bridge and knock on Astra's door. The small water sprite opens the old creaking door. I look down at her, meeting her ocean-blue eyes that match the color of her skin. "Good evening, Miss Astra!" I greet.

"Oh, Miss Edin! Good evening to you!"

"I have a delivery for you from the apothecary. It is quite heavy, may I bring it in for you?"

Astra smiles, her wrinkled skin pinching at her eyes, "That would be lovely, dear. Thank you."

I carry the crate in, sitting it down on a wooden table, and begin unloading her delivery. Astra sets out two cups, pouring me some white tea, and plops two sugar cubes in, just the way I like it. I have been delivering orders to Astra for as long as I can remember.

"You don't look a day over twenty-five, Edin," she says, handing me my cup. "Maybe in mortal years, yes," I laugh. "I recently turned one thousand years old, but who keeps count?" I raise my shoulders.

Astra throws her hands up, "Everyone keeps count until their Enlightenment," raising her eyebrows, continuing, "I assume I will see you there tomorrow night?"

I smile, as anticipation builds in my stomach at the thought of tomorrow's ceremony. "I would not miss it for all the realms," I say, finishing my tea and setting it in the basin. "Thank you, Astra. I am sure I will see you next week for another delivery," I joke, heading for the door.

"Or you may be on an entirely new adventure," Astra says with a wink.

I step out, confused by her words. "What did she mean by that?" I whisper. Astra has always been a close friend and wise in her old age, but her words leave me feeling uneasy about the Enlightenment tomorrow.

I walk back through the village in a daze, Astra's words still running through my head. I take left instead of right, walking towards the forest. The village noise fades in the distance as I step into the tree line. I follow the bright red mushrooms that grow sporadically on the moss-covered ground. One would think nothing of them unless they really look. The mushrooms create a hidden trail that leads deep into the forest. I continue following the path, twisting and turning between the trees, and pushing past branches until they finally come to a clearing. Off to the right, hidden behind two weeping willows, stands a cave. I look back, making sure I have not been followed, and pick up my pace across the clearing. I push through the flowing branches of the weeping willows and step into my own little hidden sanctuary. The pressures of life fade away as I enter the mouth of the cave.

Bioluminescent mushrooms grow in bright shades of orange, pink, and green providing me light as I walk deeper inside the cave. Purple and blue crystals form up the

rocky walls, reflecting the light and creating the most

beautiful images across the ceiling. Stepping further into

the cave, sunlight shines down from an opening above onto

a stone circle table. It is the perfect space to clear my mind

while I tend to my personal plants, which cover the table.

Vines grow down the opening, braiding in on themselves. I

push up my sleeves and stick my fingers deep in the dirt,

grounding myself. The feel of the earth beneath my nails

soothes something within me. I adore my mother's garden,

but this quiet cave gives me peace. I look over my plants,

noting their growth. I then slip on my leather gloves and

begin tending to my precious plants. Oleander, hemlock,

and wolfsbane seem to love the conditions of the cave, and

flourish here but are extremely poisonous. Over the years

here in the cave, and lots of research, I have grown to love these plants. I run my gloved finger across the oleander's petals, taking in its beauty. A voice from behind startles me, causing me to jump.

"Thought I would find you here," Blythe laughs. "Needing to get away before the Enlightenment?"

"Yes," I huff. "On a delivery today, Astra said something that really shook me."

Blythe runs her bare hand across the wolfsbane, taking advantage of her earth magic. "Astra is older than time itself, don't let her get to you," she laughs.

"Or she is possibly wise in her old age," I retort, raising my eyebrows.

"Possibly," Blythe shrugs. "Or she is insane."

I roll my eyes and turn back to my plants.

Blythe steps up beside me and asks, "Okay, what did she say?"

I breathe out and begin nervously pacing across the room. "Just that I could be on an entirely new adventure in the coming days," I mumble, picking at the dirt under my nails.

"Edin," Blythe says, laying her hand over mine, "Do not let her words get to you. Everything will be just fine, and no matter what adventure you are on, I will be by your side." Blythe pulls me in, wrapping her arms around me. I slide my arms up around her, squeezing tight.

"Thank you, Blythe."

"Of course, Love." She squeezes me tight and releases me.

"Come on, it's almost dinner time and I am sure Odessa is wondering where we are."

I look up through the skylight in the cave ceiling and see that the sky has turned shades of orange and pink. "I must have let time get away from me. It happens so easily here." I give all my plants a final drink of water and leave them until I can return tomorrow after the ceremony.

CHAPTER 11

EDIN

Blythe and I walk side by side out of the cave and back through the forest, following the trail of mushrooms. The cave has been our secret for as long as I can remember. We stumbled upon it years ago as children playing in the woods. I watch as Blythe runs her fingertips across the trees, and moss begins to grow in every place she has touched. Branches and vines lean toward her, wrapping their leaves around her hands just to say hello. I am in awe of how in tune she is with her earth magic, it is quite beautiful. We pass through the tree line as the sun completely sets. Now that I have cleared my head, I feel as though I can finally breathe again. I watch the small village of Blackburn start to glow, as the lanterns are lit one by one, by the town fire sprite. I take pride in knowing, after tomorrow, I will truly be able to contribute to this sweet little village I call home.

We walk the crowded cobblestone streets, as everyone heads home. Finally coming up to my cottage, I turn toward Blythe, "Would you like to join us for dinner?"

"Is that even a question? Of course! Odessa's cooking can't be beaten," Blythe smiles.

I unlatch the wooden gate allowing Blythe through, but she offers for me to pass first. I shrug, taking the lead. Reaching for the cottage door, it swings open before I am able to grab it.

"Edin!" Della squeals and all of my siblings come crashing to the door. "

Well, hello," I say in surprise. I look back to Blythe, and she laughs, her fox ears wiggling mischievously. "Did you know about this?" I giggle.

"Possibly," Blythe laughs.

Della pulls me through the door to the small dining room. She drags out a chair at the head of the table, "Sit, Edin," Della chirps, and everyone crowds in around me. My mother comes in with plates stacked up her arms of delicious-looking food, and my father follows behind with a massive roast. I can not help my smile, knowing this is my favorite meal.

"You did not have to do all of this," I say, as tears fill my eyes.

My mother takes a seat next to me, grabbing my hand. "I know, my sweet girl."

All seven of my siblings sit down at the table. I look down the long row and meet Blythe's stare. My heart is so full having the entire family together in one room. The clinking of glasses and light conversation bounce off the walls. Blythe winks at me, as she passes carrots on to Della. My father finishes cutting the roast and walks over to me. He kisses my forehead and takes the other seat beside me. He clears his throat and lifts his glass of mead, "To Edin," he proudly speaks, "May her enlightenment fulfill her soul."

Everyone raises their glass in unison, "To Edin."

CHAPTER 12

EDIN

Present day...

"What in all of Helheim happened last night?" I grumble as I grab my throbbing head. My mouth is so dry and my throat feels like sandpaper. That much winter wine is never a good idea. As I start to come to my senses, I take in my surroundings, noticing I am in an unfamiliar dark room with gray stone walls. I stare straight up at the recessed ceiling. There is a painted mural, depicting the castle in the Elysian sky and the fiery rivers surrounding the castle of Helheim; separating the two realms is the veil of purgatory. A beautiful wrought iron crystal chandelier hangs from the center. I toss the blankets back and turn my head around the room. The bed is outfitted in black velvet with an intricately carved wooden headboard. My world spins as I sit up, and I close my eyes hoping the revolutions will slow down. "How much did I drink last night? This has to be a dream," I mumble under my breath. Slowly, I open my eyes again, and the scenery is unchanged. The room is fit for a gothic queen, lovely and romantic in its decor. Golden ropes tie back heavy black drapes on either side of floor-to-ceiling windows. Dripping black candles are placed around the bed on tall metal candle holders. *Am I still at Swindon Castle? I was obviously too drunk to make it home last night.* I start to drag myself out of bed, noticing a dull ache between my thighs, the memories of last night come rushing to the forefront of my mind. The thought of my body being enjoyed by two men, both of whom I just met, makes my cheeks flush with heat. This explains the raw feeling in my throat and the soreness in my jaw.

Two men at once? Blythe would be so proud.

I search the room, looking for any clues as to how I came to be in this beautiful place. Just adjacent to the bedroom is a charming washroom, with stone surrounding the deep soaking tub and open shower. Soaps and shampoos line the side of the tub and fluffy white towels are set on the countertop. I shrug, hoping whoever left all this does not mind if I use them. I turn on the spray, wanting to wash the smell of stale winter wine and sex from my body. Removing my ceremony gown and turning to face the mirror, my breath catches noticing the image on my chest. "Shit. I almost forgot about my goddess mark." I touch the skin where the sword is engraved. The pain is gone and the image is flush with my skin, as if it has always been a part of my body. I quickly remove the gown, yearning for the warm water. Walking toward the shower, something catches my eye. Turning my back to the mirror, the reflection stuns me, and I stumble backward into the countertop. Lifting my black wavy hair, I crane my neck to see an image on the back of my shoulder. Two black arrows point toward each other crisscrossing at the center. I run my fingers over the skin, feeling for raised edges or scarring, but the skin is unmarred, just like my goddess mark. "What in all the realms is happening to me?" I huff. My head spins with the realization that this life is nothing like I imagined it would be. Tears sting my eyes as a sob works its way up my throat, threatening to break free. I swallow it back down, trying to take deep breaths. Stepping into the hot spray of the shower, I press my hands on the rough stone wall to brace myself from the dizzying whirlwind of my thoughts.

After bathing last night's filth from my body, which does little to scrub it from my mind, I wrap myself in a towel, reluctantly leaving the warmth of the bathroom. I search for something to wear that is a little more comfortable than my ceremony gown. Opening the doors to the wardrobe I find familiar gowns, tops, and pants. *My clothes from home? This is definitely not Swindon Castle.* There are also training leathers that do not belong to me but look to be in my size. I opt for a flowing black gown with lace adorning the sleeves and collar. I smile, remembering my mother gave me this gown as a gift for my Enlightening ceremony. The silk fabric slides over my skin, so soft that it raises goosebumps across my arms. I crack open the large double doors and peer down the long hallway. The room I am in sits at the very end. Slipping out

of the door, I begin searching for answers to my current

predicament. I creep down the hall, looking over the

painted portraits that line the walls. The faces of the

portraits seem to look back at me as I make my way down

a beautiful wrought iron staircase that empties into a den

and connects to the entryway of the castle. A large crystal

chandelier hangs from the ceiling just above a pair of

overstuffed armchairs with a roaring fire burning in a grand

stone fireplace, casting flickering light around the room.

The mantle is crafted of dark wood, almost black, with

carvings of angels and hellions along the underside.

Candles burn on bronze candelabras positioned on the wall

behind the chairs. At the back of the room prismatic light

dances across the floor and walls in a multitude of colors

leading me to a set of stained glass doors, reminding me of

my home in Blackburn. The arched doors extend to the ceiling with panes of muted blues, greens, and yellows. I walk over, opening the doors with a click. Inside is an extravagant library, row after row of old tomes line the wooden shelves and the warmth from the crackling fireplace beckons me into the room. More worn-looking armchairs are positioned around an ornate wooden table that sits in the middle of the entrance. Stacks of old leather-bound books lay across the table. The unexpected smell of freshly baked bread sweeps through the room, pulling me reluctantly out of the library, through the den, and back into the hallway.

I am certainly out of my element in this place.

CHAPTER 13

EDIN

I follow the sound of pots and pans clanging and the wonderful aroma. Pushing through a large set of doors to a kitchen, I see a mortal woman, busy at work. "Hello," I quietly say, causing the woman to jump.

Her head whips up from the counter, "Miss Edin!" she exclaims. The woman rushes over, patting her hands off on her apron. "I hope I did not wake you, Dear. Welcome to Purgatory. My name is Seraphine, but most call me Sera," she says, reaching out her hand.

My head starts spinning again as I reach to shake her hand, "It is nice to meet you Sera. Correct me if I am wrong, but did you just say Purgatory?"

Sera laughs, "Oh, but of course, my Dear. Where else would the Goddess of Purgatory reside?" I stumble over to a chair near the counter, needing to take a seat. Sera smiles, "No need to worry. I will be here full-time at Gehenna Castle, as your housemaid. I will do my best to make this an effortless transition for you, Miss Edin."

I return the smile, attempting to hide my confusion, "Thank you, Sera. I am pleased to have you here with me." Sera walks back to her station, as I attempt to comprehend the newfound knowledge. I watch Sera, as she hums to herself. She is a petite, round woman, with dimples in her cheeks and a grandmotherly air about her.

An armored guard steps into the kitchen, halting our conversation. "Miss Edin, General Osiris of the Elysian Army is waiting at the castle gates."

I smile at the guard, "Thank you, allow him to enter please, General Osiris is a…friend."

I follow behind Sera as she makes her way to the entrance of the castle. She opens the door to a handsomely familiar red-haired man, slightly calming my nerves. "Osiris," I smile.

Osiris bows, "Good morning, Edin."

I welcome him in as Sera questions, "Will you be joining us for breakfast, General Osiris?"

I answer for him, much louder than I intend to, "That would be lovely, Sera. Thank you." I wince, as my head throbs, reminding me of my hangover. We step back into the kitchen, pulling chairs up to the counter where Sera is working.

"How are you feeling this morning?" Osiris asks, giving me a wink.

"If you are referring to last night, my head is killing me and I have been dizzy since I woke up. I have a ton of questions about waking up in this strange place." "

I am here to answer all your questions," he smiles.

"And I will finish up breakfast, so you two can go out sightseeing on full stomachs," Sera chirps in, cracking an egg into the bowl.

"Oh, I was not aware we had plans today," I say, raising an eyebrow at Osiris.

He chuckles, "I thought I would show you around the village today, and let you get a feel for your new realm."

"I would love to see the village and meet the people of Purgatory." Needing answers, I set aside my nerves, asking, "Do either of you know how I arrived here? I would like to no longer be in the dark if you do not mind."

Sera cracks another egg into a bowl, nodding to Osiris, "Osirus carried you in last night after your spill at the ceremony, such a gentleman."

Osirus raises his eyebrows at me with a smirk, "Nasty spill you took at the Enlightenment," he says. I giggle, knowing what happened last night was definitely not a spill. "I also had a few things from Blackburn sent over for you, so you would feel more at home."

I am taken aback, "*You* packed my things?"

Osiris raises his hands as if he is surrendering, "Before you go thinking I rummaged through your wardrobe, I had attendants meet with your family so everything could be packed properly."

"Oh," I laugh, "Well, thank you."

Sera finishes with breakfast, setting the last of it on the table. Eggs, bacon, toast, and fruit preserves are piled high on silver platters. My mouth waters and I realize how hungry I am. As we eat breakfast, we chat about what my role will be in Purgatory. Osiris explains my duties of casting judgment on the souls who cross over to this realm. He continues on about necromancy and how I will have the ability to commune with the dead and see the events in their lives that may or may not condemn their souls.

"You will also be able to raise your own army. You will have the power to bend the will of the dead into becoming your obedient soldiers." Osiris adds while taking another bite of eggs.

"Let's hope that doesn't happen. We haven't had a war in over two millenniums," Sera adds from where she stands, cleaning up the last of the breakfast mess.

Between bites, Osiris says, "I do apologize, ladies, being a part of the military, I am always on guard." His embarrassment shows in his expression, and it is rather adorable.

"All of this sounds quite daunting. How will I learn to use my newly acquired magic?"

"The King of Helheim is sending someone here to train you," Osiris blurts out.

I almost choke on my toast, coughing. "I assumed *you* would be my trainer?" I ask in astonishment.

"I would love that, but unfortunately my duties to Elysia keep me quite busy. Even so, I will be here to assist you in any way I can."

"I appreciate your kindness, Osiris."

"Now go get changed so we can head out to the village," he says, giving me a wink.

I return to my room to change, trying to shake the nagging feeling I have about my training. I select a simple black dress with a tie at the waist and a slit up both legs, so

I will be able to move easier. I look over all of the familiar gowns, touching the fabric. An empty, longing feeling creeps into the pit of my stomach, making me miss Blackburn, the only home I have ever known. Tears begin to well in the corners of my eyes. I quickly blink them away, refusing to think of home and all that I am missing right now. Today is about starting my journey here in my new role and I need to make the best of it. I braid my hair loosely, leaving wavy strands out to frame my face. I finish my look with simple flat shoes and a purple cloak, attempting to dress more like a goddess. I check over myself in the mirror, before heading back down to the kitchen.

CHAPTER 14

ENDRICKS

"ENDRICKS!" my father roars. "What in all of Helheim were you thinking, pulling a stunt like that?" King Adonis snarls, sending his fist through the stone wall.

"Father, calm down. Am I not allowed to have the smallest bit of pleasure as heir to the throne?" I chuckle, the look on his face telling me he is not amused.

"At the Enlightenment, of all places, you decide to consort with the Goddess of Purgatory," King Adonis growls, sending another fist through the wall, barely missing my head.

"Consorting is such a strong word, I was just playing with my newfound pet," I say.

He grabs a hold of my collar, yelling, "She is the Goddess of Purgatory, not your pet. We have an age-old alliance with the overseer of Purgatory, that I plan to keep; and as my son and only heir, you will work to strengthen that alliance. Do I need to repeat your orders from our council?" he spits.

Brushing my father off haphazardly I say, "No father," before making my way out.

My father has ruled Helheim with an iron fist for thousands of years, and I plan to do the same. I am the king's assassin, not a babysitter. I am not sure why it became my job to stay in the new Goddess's good graces in the first place. There will always be vile, cruel souls in this world, and it will be her job to judge them. It is my job to carry out their deserved torture here in Helheim. I slam the door open to my study to see Oren, a fire sprite and my footman, respectfully waiting for me. Oren has been a loyal subject of mine since I was little.

"Oren!"

"Yes, my lord?" Oren stutters, standing at attention while awaiting my order.

"Have my things been packed?" I question.

Looking at his list with a contented smirk, Oren responds "Yes, my lord. We will cross through the veil to Purgatory in one day's time."

CHAPTER 15

OSIRIS

I watch as Edin returns, descending the staircase. The same spark I felt at the Enlightenment runs through my chest, making my heart rate pick up. I force myself to pull my stare from her gorgeous golden eyes and the way her wavy black hair falls across her face. Opening the door I ask, "Are you ready for this new adventure, Goddess of Purgatory?" I watch the shocked expression turn to curiosity as she takes in the new scenery. We make our way down the stairs and walk through the castle gates.

"Osiris?" Edin asks.

"Yes?" Edin's face turns sullen, "Is Sera forced to work in the castle because she is mortal?"

"Oh no! Not in the slightest. The mortal people of Purgatory choose to stay in this realm, as it is an honor to serve a god or goddess so closely. It is the place that they fit best since they are unable to gain any magical powers. Some even request to be sent to Elysia or Helheim to serve. They are highly regarded by many, and known as essential to making things run smoothly."

"Oh," Edin's expression shifts back to curiosity, looking through the mist as the village comes into view.

Cobblestone buildings line the village south of Gehenna Castle. The deteriorating structures are home to the villagers patiently waiting for their soul's sentence from their new Goddess. "My villagers live in these?" Edin mutters.

"The dwellings are only temporary for the current villagers. Just a pit stop," I say, trying to make light of the situation.

"As soon as my training is complete, this will be my first task. Even if it is only for a moment, they deserve better than this," Edin says, casting her arm out towards the village.

I smile, "Spoken like a true Goddess."

The overcast weather is placid, remaining unaffected by time. Trees never grow and a fog that blankets everything never seems to lift. Old, faded, and moth-eaten curtains hang in open windows creating a ghostly ambiance. Oddly, flowers bloom throughout, bringing a pop of color to the dreary village.

"Tulips," Edin smiles.

"They are quite beautiful," I respond, picking a couple and handing them to her.

She brings one to her nose, "Tulips are my favorite."

"How fitting," I chuckle, "These tulips are also known as Queen of the Night, for the deep maroon, almost black, petals."

She giggles, "I would say so with my new title." Edin's smile fades as her eyes drift to the left of the houses. Up on the hill, chains dangle in mid-air, holding one large shackle a piece.

I point towards the chains, "The previous God of Purgatory would keep the villagers with the cruelest souls chained up to keep them away from the innocent ones.

That will be up to you as soon as you can wield your magic."

Edin rubs her forehead, "I did not even think about the criminals." She quickly pulls her eyes back to the village. Villagers mill around in the streets moving away when they catch sight of us. We spot several peeking out of their windows trying to catch a glimpse of the Goddess as we move along side by side, taking in the desolate wasteland that is Purgatory.

"We must have seen fifty people so far. Why do they shy away from us?" Edin asks, noticing the onlookers.

"Well even though you may not look frightening, they may be a bit intimidated." She scrunches her nose at my suggestion. "Edin, you cast the final word about where their soul will be housed for all eternity. So if they have lived a life of crime and corruption, they are most likely going to be inclined to stay away from you as long as they can," I shrug. "You know, to prolong their judgment day."

Edin laughs, "Oh please, if anything they are shying away from you. You are the towering man in full uniform with an eight-foot wingspan. I am just an unassuming Nephilim from Blackburn," she teases, giving me a wink.

We stroll along for some time, making our acquaintance with the few villagers who are brave enough to approach us, only offering a few words.

"Welcome Goddess, I hope you are settling in well here," a large Taurus says as he takes a bow in front of Edin.

"Thank you, sir," she says before he scurries off to hide in one of the houses nearby.

A villager with ragged stumps poking out of her back, asks, "Hello Miss, do you know when you will start casting out our sentences?" She gives a sickeningly sweet smile, making me want to shield Edin from whatever plans this obviously deplorable fallen angel is contemplating.

Edin clears her throat, seeming to search for the correct words to give the fallen angel, "I have yet to start my training and do not have much information for you, but I can say with assurance that I will work hard to get through training quickly and ascend to my seat as your Goddess."

The fallen angel scrunches her face and mumbles, "Well don't try too hard, some of us would rather be here than where you are going to send us." She then looks up at me and smiles slyly, "Feel free to visit anytime you like, warrior." She gives me a wink as she sashays away, her robe swishing as she walks toward her shanty.

Edin looks at me with her mouth open, "Did that female just come onto you?" she laughs.

"It seems that way. Are you jealous?" I tease, as I offer her my arm. She swats at me playfully as we make our way to the outskirts of the settlement.

"No, *General,* you are free to have relations with whoever pleases you," she says, her words dripping with sarcasm.

"Well Miss *Goddess,* I am quite content with my current station," I say, taking in her beautiful smile. Her cheeks turn bright red as she giggles, holding my arm a little tighter.

We find a flat grassy area to rest for a bit before we head back to the castle. We are situated near the Deadwoods, a wooded area crowded with withered trees. Black bark and tall crooked branches remind me of long demon hands reaching toward the sky. Not exactly picturesque, but it is the only thing in Purgatory that resembles a landscape.

"How are you feeling about your first day with your new assignment?" I ask as I lay my coat on the ground for us to sit on.

"I miss my home, my family, and my best friend, Blythe, but I really appreciate you being here to ease me into this new chapter of my life," she says, looking out over the trees.

"There is no need to thank me, I am no stranger to loneliness. I know so much has changed for you in such a short amount of time, Edin. You will learn the ropes soon, I am sure. For now, let's just get you acclimated with your new position." I say, patting her arm.

CHAPTER 16

EDIN

Sitting next to me, Osiris is close enough that our thighs touch. "Tell me about your home," he says.

"There's not much to tell really. We live in a cottage in a little village called Blackburn. It is rather beautiful though, my grandparents built it many years ago. There are stained glass windows that my grandmother crafted by hand, and wooden planters out front. Our garden is vast with herbs and flowers as far as you can see. It is modest, but it is my favorite place in the world." My eyes cloud over with tears, homesickness is not something I have ever experienced before, not like this.

"I can tell with the way your eyes light up when you talk about it," Osiris smiles down at me.

"It sounds wonderful. How did you meet Blythe?"

"We have been friends since I can remember. There is not a time in my memory that she was not a part of my life. Well, until now. I feel so detached from the life I had just yesterday." I can no longer hold back the tears that have been threatening to spill from my eyes.

Osiris reaches up and gently wipes my cheeks with the back of his fingers, "Things will get easier, Edin. Do not worry, you will see your family and friends again very soon. Do not think of this as the end of your life but as a new chapter." I give Osiris a small smile. A low blood curdling growl comes out from the darkness of the forest as I go to lay my head on his shoulder.

CHAPTER 17

OSIRIS

We swing our heads toward the Deadwoods as a group of hellhounds emerge slowly out of the trees, heads lowered, and teeth bared. Bright orange flames writhe from their bodies, sprouting out of their black, leathery skin. Their growls seemingly add fuel to their flames, immersing more of their bodies with each show of rage. The hounds start to fan out as they come closer to our resting spot. I slowly get up into a fighting stance, taking Edin by the arm and moving her behind me. Raising my hand, aiming it towards the hellhounds, I yell, "Configure," and warp reality, creating a diversion. The wind swirls around us and sharp antlers begin to manifest from out of the dust. A body starts to take shape, glowing bright. My configuration takes the full form of a large glowing elk standing between us and the hounds.

"Chaos magic," I hear Edin mumble from over my shoulder.

The ethereal elk darts towards the hounds, bucking at the pack and pulling their attention away from us. From the tree line, I watch as another hellhound creeps out of the woods with the same black skin, but black flames consume its body. My stomach drops. "We are outnumbered," I grunt, glancing back at Edin.

The black flamed hound approaches from behind the pack, who still have their attention trained on the elk. In an instant, he pounces on the largest of the hounds in the group, startling them out of their trance. The pack turns their attention to the black flaming hound, snapping and growling. From the other side of the tree line, another hellhound stalks out of the woods. I assume he must be the alpha of the group from how he has laid back in waiting until this point. The leader keeps his keen eyes trained on me, and I meet his stare. Suddenly, he lunges forward at full speed. Jerking my sword from its scabbard, I slash at the beast just missing his neck, slicing his right shoulder. Flaming, liquid-like magma seeps from the gash, melting the side of my blade. The hound slings his head towards the ground, snapping at my leg. Its teeth barely graze my leg, but tear through my pants causing me to lose my footing as I hit the dirt.

"No!" Edin screams. She throws her hands out trying to catch me as purple electrical orbs fly from her hands. The ground shakes when the orbs hit the earth, causing the surface to crumble and crack. Confusion streaks her face and she stumbles back, looking down at her palms. Without hesitation, I jump back to my feet, flipping my grasp and driving the still-sharpened edge of my sword up toward the beast's chest as it steps back from the crumbling earth. I feel the blade slide between his ribs, all the way to the hilt and out through his spine. A loud yelp escapes the hound as he gasps for air. I shove its body off the blade of my sword, flaming blood slinging onto the back of my hand. I let out a roar of pain looking down at my ruined flesh. Tendons and bone become visible as the thin skin burns away. The rest of the pack looks over the dead alpha's body and back to the hound wreathed in black flames. They begin to retreat, escaping into the cover of the trees.

Edin whips her cloak off, wiping the burning substance from my hand as best she can. She rips a strip of clean cloth from the cloak and wraps my ruined hand. "We need to get back to the castle so I can tend to your wound properly," Edin says, as she gathers my coat. I watch the black flamed hound dip back into the tree line. "

I think that would be the best plan of action," I snarl, motioning toward the trees where the creatures try to hide.

CHAPTER 18

EDIN

We quickly make our way through the village and up the cobblestone path, entering the castle gates. I swing open the doors, yelling for Sera. "I need two clean water basins, bandages, and rags, please."

"Of course, Miss Edin," Sera says in a rush.

"Osiris, go have a seat in the den. I will be right back," I motion towards the den while I head straight to my room for my store of Mother's healing salve. I rush back and begin removing my torn cloak from his hand, causing him to wince. Dipping his hand into the cool water to wash away the remaining corrosive substance, I can feel his eyes on me as I work. I ignore the familiar shock running up my arm as I clean his wound. "This salve will heal your wounds in no time. You may feel a sting at first, but it will subside quickly." I explain, applying the cream in a thick layer over his ruined skin.

Osiris grabs the arm of the chair, bracing for the pain. I hear the unmistakable sound of splintering wood as the pain jolts through his wound. "Gods!" He grinds out, "That is some powerful salve!" I gingerly take his hand, blowing on it until he relaxes and releases the arm of the chair. As I apply another bandage, tying it gently, Osiris reaches toward my face, tucking a stray strand of hair behind my pointed ear. "You were quite something out there, Edin," he says, with admiration in his eyes.

"What?" I laugh, continuing to wrap the bandage, "You were the one who fended off hounds with your fighting prowess. I did nothing, but stand behind you in shock."

He tilts his head, "Many decisions could have been made, and under that type of pressure, you can only make the right one. You chose to stay calm, never screaming, and when I was down you were able to distract the hounds. That is quite brave in my eyes, never running from the enemy. You must meet them at their level."

At a loss for words I am frozen, looking down at my palms again, "I am still unsure of what even happened back there."

CHAPTER 19

OSIRIS

"It takes time and practice to learn the way your magic works and how to use it. It has not quite been a day yet and you have already been able to create a distraction. That is an amazing feat, showing that you are very in tune with your power," I gently tilt her chin and make her look up at me. "Success is the sum of small efforts, repeated day in and day out. Repeat that to yourself anytime you feel discouraged," I say, staring into her beautiful golden eyes. Edin takes a deep breath and slowly lets it out. I pull her toward me and look down at her lips. "You are unbelievable, Edin," I whisper and close the gap between us gently pressing my lips to hers. When our lips connect I get that jolt of electricity that happens every time she touches me. I am beginning to crave that feeling. Pulling away slowly I hold her face in my hands, "I am sorry, but I do have to leave for tonight, I have some things to take care of in Elysia."

Disappointment creeps across her face, "When will you return?"

"Tomorrow afternoon. I promise," I wink, "You will have to tell me more about your home and Blythe tomorrow. Maybe over dinner?" I ask, helping Edin up off the floor.

"That sounds lovely," she says, fixing her skirt and then walking with me to the door.

I hold her hand, rubbing my thumb across the back of hers, as we say our goodbyes. Bending down to give her one last kiss, I pull her close to my chest and press my lips to hers.

Gods, I could kiss her for all eternity if she would allow it. I reluctantly release her and reach for the door.

"We will have to do this again," she says, with a playful grin, "With less danger and wild hellhounds, of course."

I laugh, "We will pick up where we left off as soon as I return. Goodbye for a little while, Edin." She smiles up at me and lets go of my hand. I hold on to her for a moment longer, taking in her beauty, and then I make my way out of the castle, all the while wishing I never had to leave.

CHAPTER 20

EDIN

Closing the castle door, I lean back on it with a huff, "What a day." The thought of the library comes to mind. "Maybe there is a book that will help explain this power." I head straight for the library. Pushing open the stained glass doors, another thought comes to the forefront. *The mark on my shoulder.* I walk over to the table mesmerized by the quaint beauty of the library. Handling the books carefully, as they look as though they might disintegrate in my hands, I begin looking over the covers. "*The History of Helheim,* " I read aloud, "*Purgatory 101, The Avernus, and Records of Celestial Beings and Spirits.*" I continue to thumb through the titles, so many are about the history and inner workings of Purgatory. I feverishly search for a tome about glyphs or markings given by the gods. Turning a few over, a dust plume balloons up causing me to cough and my eyes to water. I fan away the cloud and there at the bottom of the stack is a tattered leather-bound relic titled *Record of Runes*. I pick it up carefully, flipping through its thin pages. Searching through the many symbols and their meanings, I finally land on what seems to be an exact drawing of my tattoo. I trace the arrow's point with my finger until it intersects with the other, reading the excerpt underneath. "The mark of love: appearing after two, adult, fated mates come into contact. The two souls intertwine becoming one, conjoining both life forces, extending their life expectancy. The union increases both mates' magical abilities, as well as creating a magnetic bond between the two in which both mates may feel each other's pain. Although it is an uncommon occurrence, it is an otherworldly connection. "

My heart stops, as my breath catches in my throat. I stare at the pages dumbfounded, wishing that I had time magic so I could go back and never open the book. Panicking, I flip through the pages faster, trying to find another picture that resembles my mark. "I must not be remembering it correctly." I find similar marks, but curved filigree surrounds the arrows or there is only one arrow. No other mark matches mine, none except the fated mate mark. "Shit," I groan, closing the book.

This can not be true! How can I be fated to another? I have just received my powers. It is not uncommon to hear of mated pairs in our culture, my parents happen to be fated. Yet, it is one of those things that you dream about when you are little. You imagine being mated to a handsome prince who sweeps you off your feet and you both ride off into the sunset on the back of a dragon. The only new beings I was in contact with last night was the King of Windemere...gross, he must be at least twenty thousand years old. Osiris, and the masked man. Shit.

"Oh Gods!*"* I huff. The image of Osiris comes into my mind. The memory of him sitting behind me, holding my hips and pumping in and out of me. I have to clench my thighs to calm the aching pulse between them. "I think I could handle that for eternity," I say, tilting my head. The masked man storms into my thoughts, looking down at me as he fucked my face. I shiver, "Oh Gods! What have I done?" Plopping myself down in an armchair, I lay my head in my hands. My mind swims with so many questions.

I have a fated mate. Does the male also gain a mark? I thought I would be able to choose the person I would be spending my life with.

My head nods forward and I startle myself awake, feeling as if I am falling. *I must have been sitting here for hours.* Getting up from the table I force myself to close the books. I will have to do more research another night. I need to sleep. Dragging myself up the stairs to my room feels like climbing a mountain after the day I have had. I sluggishly push through the door and change into a nightgown with my eyes half shut. I am finally able to crawl between the sheets, and I let out a soft moan as my body sinks into the feather mattress. My tense shoulders relax and my eyes fall shut. I drift off almost immediately, my mind too tired to think.

CHAPTER 21

EDIN

Waking to the distinct smell of coffee and bacon, the sun streams in the windows while Sera busily sets a tray of food on the side table.

"Good morning, dear," Sera says, smiling her usual wide smile that wrinkles the edges of her eyes and brightens the room.

"Good morning, Sera," I hoarsely say, despite wanting to reciprocate her liveliness.

"You seem to have had a late night, so I thought I would bring breakfast to you, today," Sera smiles, positioning the pillows behind me, propping me up in bed, and goes back to her breakfast tray.

"You are sent from Elysia itself, Sera," I thank her and take the coffee she offers me. I savor the first sip of the hot liquid as it replenishes my soul and wakes my mind. Sera's coffee is the best I have ever tasted, with hints of hazelnut and dark chocolate. She works her own type of magic in that kitchen every day. She brings the tray of food and sets it over my lap. My stomach growls loudly as I look over the massive plate. After the attack last night and tending to Osiris's wound, I did not even think to eat dinner. Between bites, I ask Sera, "I was thinking of exploring the castle today. Is there anywhere in particular I should venture?"

She busies herself, placing a log on the fire, "Well, there is the alchemy tower over on the east corner, I bet you would find it especially interesting since you have a background in healing."

I finish up breakfast and dress quickly. Then, I take my tray and plates back to the kitchen and wash them so Sera does not have to, the woman does enough for me. I make my way to the east side of the castle, walking under the beautiful stone archways adorned with intricate carvings of vines and flowers lining the wall. At the end of the hall is a spiral staircase leading straight up. I take the wrought iron handrail and make my way up toward the sky.

As I reach the top, I find myself in a room with shelves lining every wall. I am in awe at the multitude of glass vials, jars, books, and plants on every shelf. A railing above the shelves runs around the ceiling. On one side is a ladder that slides the length of the room, giving access to even the very top shelves, which are high above my head. The countertops run across the room. Potted plants I am familiar with from my home crowd most of the area. I glance over the plants, noting the poisonous ones sitting high up on the shelf to the left. Oleander and wolfsbane are placed far out of reach, and for good reason. The two poisonous plants remind me of my little hidden garden in the cave back in Blackburn. The familiar scent of lavender and peppermint invades my senses and my mind is transported to my family's garden in early summer, running through the rows of lavender. Remembering the feel of the sun on my face and my bare feet on the cool earth brings tears to my eyes. I let them fall, missing my home so much it hurts. I pluck a sprig of lavender, sniffing its sweet herbal scent. I walk to the window and look out over the land of purgatory. The sun is midway in the sky, and I can see the village, with all its dilapidated houses, all the way to the Deadwoods with its finger-like branches reaching up toward the sky. I sigh, taking in the view. There is a certain beauty here that I failed to see before.

The sound of footsteps startles me, I whirl around to see Darian, the doorman, emerging from the staircase.

"Pardon me, Miss Edin," Darian says, breathlessly, "General Osiris is here to see you."

"Thank you, Darian, would you send him up to me, please?"

"Certainly, Goddess."

Darian disappears down the stairs and I go back to investigating the jars of oils along the wall noticing their tiny labels. I find a stash of empty jars and then painstakingly scan the labels of the many vials until I have gathered the ingredients for my mother's healing salve. I mix tea tree and chamomile oils together, adding a bit of crushed lavender from the sprig I picked earlier. Then, I light a burner that sits atop the counter and melt some beeswax. Finally, I slowly stir in the oil mixture while the beeswax is hot. I mix until the salve is a creamy honey color, smooth save for the flecks of lavender. Just as I am pouring the tincture into a jar, I hear Osiris's unmistakably heavy footsteps ascending the spiral staircase.

"Good morning, Osiris," I smile at him as his body emerges from below the floor.

"Good afternoon, Edin."

"Is it afternoon already? I have spent all morning up here."

"Is this your new favorite room in the castle?" he asks with a wink, grinning.

"I love it. It reminds me of home," I say looking around the room. "Oh, I made this for you." I offer Osiris the jar of salve.

He takes it, looking it over with curiosity, "Thank you, but what is it?" "

My mother's healing salve, for any time you are wounded and I am not around."

He takes my hand and kisses it, "You never cease to amaze me."

"I thought you could use a little of me while you are away." I look up into his stormy-gray eyes.

"Trust me, Edin, when I am away it is difficult to think of anything, but you." The sweet moment is cut off by my stomach loudly rumbling. "It seems you are overdue for lunch," Osiris chuckles, and takes me by the hand, leading me down the stairs and toward the kitchen.

As we walk through the kitchen doors we are greeted by the sight of Sera adding sandwiches and fruit to a basket. "I thought you two could use some fresh air, so I packed a picnic for you. There is everything you will need in this basket for a respectable lunch, including some sparkling wine and glasses," Sera winks, handing the basket over to Osiris.

"You are so thoughtful, Sera. Thank you," I say as my stomach rumbles again at the thought of food.

"Oh, it's nothing dear. You two have fun!" Sera says as she waves us out the door.

We venture down to the garden in front of the castle, looking for a flat spot. Osiris sets the basket down on a hill that overlooks the village on the east side of the castle grounds. The sun is high in the sky and feels lovely on my bare shoulders. He spreads the blanket and kneels down, laying out the food for each of us, making sure to hand out my food first in a chivalrous fashion.

"Where did you learn to be such a gentleman," I laugh, taking a grape and popping it into my mouth.

He pours a glass of wine and hands it over to me. Smirking, he pours himself a glass, "I just learned over the years how to treat a woman."

"Oh," I drag out, "Are there many women in your past, General?" I ask, and my stomach turns as the words leave my mouth. The question makes me realize I do not really know much about this man at all.

"No, I have never had much time for courtship. My etiquette was taught by the Elysian army. Women are served first during group meals and the men do the serving. It is a form of respect. In most instances the women are the leaders and captains of the soldiers, therefore respect is given not only due to gender, but also rank."

I feel the wine warming my insides, "So you never had a relationship with one of these women warriors?"

His sheepish smile gives away his answer before he even speaks, "I did fill a lonely night or two with women in the military, but it never progressed to anything serious."

"Understandable," I shrug, "What about before?"

"I knew a girl then that I always seemed to be drawn to. We would pass each other in school or see each other in the market, but I was never brave enough to talk to her." Osiris chuckles, running his fingers through his hair. "I was a wisp of a boy as a child. The girls did not pay much attention to me. Why do you ask?"

I stare at him in disbelief, "I find it hard to believe that *you* were not attractive in your youth." I motion to his body, allowing my eyes to linger on his broad chest. My cheeks burn as I meet his eyes again, and he smiles at me knowingly.

"I did not look this way until the army whipped me into shape. I had a grueling training schedule that I have continued over the years." He takes a bite of his sandwich, and I follow suit, needing something on my stomach to weaken the effects of the wine. "What about you? Have you had any serious relationships over the years back in Blackburn?" he asks between bites.

Wanting to take my time to mull over his question, I take a bite of my lunch and chew slowly. "I have had a few amorous entanglements here and there but, like you, none were very serious." A blush creeps into my cheeks as the memory of the night with Osiris and the masked man invades my mind. I disguise my reaction by taking another bite of my sandwich.

"I think your bashfulness is adorable." Osiris laughs, setting down his wine glass.

"Stop teasing me," I giggle at him.

"I am serious. Your gold eyes light up when you blush."

Of course, his compliment causes my blush to deepen. "What would your fellow warriors think of sweet and chivalrous Osiris?" I mockingly swoon and then wink at him.

"I reserve this side of me for only you, Edin." I hide my smile, taking another sip of my wine.

I lean back on the blanket, watching the sky turn from blue to shades of purple and orange. "If you had not joined the military, what would you have done with yourself," I question, rolling onto my stomach.

Osiris lays back next to me and scratches his head. "Gods, I have never thought beyond the military. It has been my entire life," he huffs.

I pick at the grass, giggling, "You could have been a rover, traveling through all the realms."

"Possibly," he chuckles. Osiris tugs on my arm, and I roll toward him, leaning on his chest. "I am thankful for the dark path I have walked because it has led me here to you," he says, brushing the hair from my face.

Electricity runs through me, and my stomach fills with butterflies. I place my hand on his chest, lean in, and kiss Osiris. I pull back, whispering, "I am thankful as well."

Running his fingers through my hair, he pulls me back in, and our lips meet. Osiris rolls over, and I land on my back, lips still pressed together. I drag my hand up his tunic, grabbing him by the collar, and pulling him even closer. Our kiss becomes more passionate, and I can not help but nip at his lip.

Osiris breaks the kiss, chuckling, "Feisty Little Hellion."

I can not help but laugh as I smile up at him.

A gust of wind sweeps through, causing me to shiver. I look around realizing the sun has now set. Osiris sits up, and extends his hand to me, "Come on, let us get a better view of the sky." I smile up at him, grabbing the blanket from under me as I stand.

I follow behind Osiris and he pulls me through the castle garden. He swings open a wrought iron gate and I slip through as it shuts behind me. Roses of every color grow wildly, trailing up the side of the castle wall. We walk under a trellis, and I watch as Osiris takes out his dagger and cuts a rose from the vine. He quickly slices the thorns from the stem and offers it to me, "It is no tulip."

I take the rose in my hand, pulling it to my nose, "It is beautiful."

Osiris kisses my forehead, "Just like you." He takes my hand once again and pushes the vines to the side with the other. "Through here," he nods. A spiral staircase comes into view, leading high up to a large balcony.

CHAPTER 22

OSIRIS

We reach the top of the steps, and I pull Edin over to a bench stacked with pillows. She sits down, and I wrap the blanket around her. I plop down beside her, "Enough about me." I say, grabbing her chin, "Tell me about your family. I assume you were very close?"

Edin smiles, but her eyes become foggy with tears that do not fall. "Where do I even begin? I am one of eight children. So, you can imagine how hectic our house was," Edin laughs. I lean back, watching her light up as she goes on about her family. "I have five older brothers, who have always been quite protective of me, and two sisters. Della is the youngest, and she is such a ham. I think she was more excited than I was for my enlightenment. She would climb up and jump on top of me every morning, counting down the days." Joy streaks her face as her hands move wildly while she talks. "My mother, Odessa, is the kindest, sweetest soul a being could ever meet. I get my Nephilim traits from her," Edin points towards her pointed ears and small black horns. "And I would like to think I get my humor from my father, Ronan. It is quite dark, in the funniest of ways."

I chuckle, "I could see that. They all sound so lovely."

Her excitement fades, "They are wonderful. I am so thankful for all of them." Edin looks up at the night sky, sighing, "I never realized how beautiful the stars are here in Purgatory." She snorts, "Actually, I am surprised I can see the stars at all here."

I lay my arm around her shoulder, gazing up, "Even though we are in a different realm, we are all a part of the same universe." I point up at Ursa Major, "Your family could be staring up at the same constellation as we are right now."

Edin lays her head on my shoulder. "I love that." I pull her tight against my side, and she looks up at me, "Thank you, Osiris." I can not help but smile down at her.

CHAPTER 23

EDIN

I tilt my head, questioning, "Yesterday, you said you were no stranger to loneliness. What did you mean?"

Osiris looks away for a moment, wincing as if he is in pain, "I lost my parents at a very young age, and I have no siblings or family that I know of." Sadness clouds his gray eyes.

"Oh Gods, Osiris. I am so sorry to hear that. I should not have pried."

He chuckles, "It is okay, Edin. I want to share these things with you." Osiris intertwines his fingers with mine.

"What happened to your parents?"

His face becomes more solemn, and he clears his throat. "I have never really told anyone in detail what happened that night," his words catch in his throat. "But, if you want, it is easier to show you than tell you."

I nod my head, "If you are comfortable with that, but how?"

"With my chaos magic, I am able to create illusions. Just as I created the elk in front of hellhounds. I am also able to control one's mind and manipulate their vision."

I pick at my nail nervously, "Oh."

He lays his hand on my shoulder, "It is not all chaos, it can be beautiful as well. During battles, I was able to manipulate the minds of my dying soldiers and show them their family as they took their dying breath."

I reach up and rub his hand, "That is very honorable of you, Osiris. If you are truly comfortable, I will happily oblige."

Osiris lays his hands on my cheeks, "Close your eyes," he whispers, "Evoke."

I feel a rush of power run through my temples as a bright light glows behind my eyelids. My world transforms instantly to a field of tall grass. "Where are we?" I whisper.

"They can not hear you," Osiris nods towards the house. "We are in Elysia, two millennia ago."

Candlelight flickers from the windows of a small cottage in the center of the field. A red-haired man fights against the armor-clad warriors trying to drag him from his home. They force the man to his knees. The soldier behind him rips his hair back, exposing his neck, and holds a knife to his throat as he thrashes in the dirt, trying to break free. They drag a screaming woman from the cottage, pushing her to her knees in front of the red-haired man. The man jerks and kicks as the soldiers force him to watch another gut the woman from sternum to pelvis. He lowers his head, sobbing and pleading, but his cries are cut short as they slit his throat.

I hear a whimper to my right and look over. A young boy kneels in the garden as he watches the scene. Tears stream down his cherubic cheeks from his beautiful, yet familiar, grey eyes. I feel as if I have been hit in the stomach, realizing that this is Osiris. My heart breaks for him, knowing he witnessed his parents' ruthless slaughter, his entire world torn from his little hands. I reach out to console him, but my fingers slip through the vision-like mist. My stomach clenches, and I fall to my knees, heaving.

When I open my eyes, I am back on the balcony in Purgatory. Tears pour from my eyes as I gasp for air.

Osiris lays a hand on my back as I try to calm myself, "It is okay. You are here in Purgatory."

I look up at him, choking out, "It was so real, like it was happening now. I am so sorry, Osiris. I should not have asked you to relive that."

He pulls me to my feet, "No need to apologize, it was so long ago. It was my nightmare to share, and it feels like a weight has been lifted by sharing it with someone. Thank you, Edin."

"Were they just brutes that went around killing innocent people?" I am finally able to breathe normally again, although I still taste bile in the back of my throat. I sit down next to him, trying to hold it together.

"My parents were on the side of the rebels during the War of Realms. They fought back against the King of Windemere, who wanted to rule all the realms for himself. They were planning an attack against a nearby war camp, and a soldier spotted them spying one night. He followed them home." He hesitates, taking a deep breath, "My mother and father saw their torch lights, but it was too late to escape. She told me to run while they distracted the soldiers, but I could not leave them. I stood frozen in fear, watching."

I lay my hand on his, "You were just a child, Osiris."

"I should have done something," he grinds out with tears in his eyes.

"That should not have happened to you. No one should have to endure such a tragedy. You are a very strong man, Osiris."

He smiles down at me sadly, continuing, "The war lasted for years. At that time, I took refuge with a nearby blacksmith who lived alone, never having kids of his own. He was generous enough to take me in and feed me, but he never was much of the nurturing type. So, as soon as I was old enough, I left to join the Elysian army. I was trained in combat, starting out as a low-ranked soldier and eventually moving to General of my own troops." A cold breeze sweeps through, making me shiver, and my teeth start to chatter. Osiris notices, saying, "Let's take our conversation inside and get you warm," he pulls me towards the doors, which appear to lead us into the library.

Osiris lights the fireplace and settles into the overstuffed couch with me. Trying to make light of our last conversation, I say, "Tell me about Elysia, what is it like there? I have read a bit about it in my lessons, but I am sure the books do not do it justice."

"Ah, the Golden City of Invention. The bright blue skies are constantly swirling with shades of pink and orange, like a sunset. The radiant Elysium Castle sits high up in the clouds. Glass hot air balloons float overhead, beautifully crafted with intricate gold metal baskets hanging from them. Elysia is home to some of the realm's greatest minds, always creating new technology to better all the realms, like the steam train. The train was built solely to run on water. It travels all across the vast land from cities to the citadel. Each building in the city was methodically built with carvings on each door to honor the gods and adorned with decorative elements to catch the sunlight."

"Hot air balloons and sunset skies all of the time sound beautiful," I gasp.

"I could take you there one day," Osiris offers.

I nod my head enthusiastically, "Of course, I would love to see it. How do you even muster the will to leave? It sounds so glorious."

He leans in, tucking my hair behind my pointed ear, "Well, my current duty is here with you, and I am growing quite fond of this view."

The shock of electricity runs through my body as I meet his stare.

CHAPTER 24

OSIRIS

***

I pause, taking in her golden eyes that remind me of home, then close the distance, softly kissing her. Edin kisses me back, laying her hand on my cheek. I pull away as the shock wave travels through me. Edin smashes her lips to mine hungrily. I reciprocate her kiss, pushing my tongue between her lips. The back and forth of our mouths is frantic, leaving us both panting. Breaking our kiss, I slide my hands under her, cupping her ass with both hands. I pick her up, heading straight for the table. Her vanilla clove scent invades my senses. My hands sink deeper into her hips, and I pull her toward me, pressing her into my hard cock. Edin wraps her legs around me, grinding. I slide all the books onto the floor, setting her down on the table.

Grabbing her chin, I tilt her head back and kiss her deeper this time. She moans into my mouth, and I am completely overtaken by her arousal. "Are you ready for me, Edin?" I ask, between kisses.

She looks up at me through heavily lidded eyes, giving me the one word I want to hear, "Yes," she whispers breathlessly.

I untie the sash on her dress and slide it up to her hips. She is so wet that the table is slick where she sits, and my restraint breaks at the sight of her. I slide her ass to the edge of the table and bend down to lick straight up her center, tasting her. "Lift your ass for me, Edin," I growl. With her pussy level with my face, I grab her hips and pull her toward me. As I dip my tongue between her legs again, she bucks, grinding hard against my mouth. I suck and tease until her legs start to shake, and she cries out for release.

"Please, Osiris," she moans, wiggling her hips.

Releasing her ass, I untie the laces to my pants and spring my throbbing cock free. Positioning myself at her entrance I push into her slowly and stop, feeling her tight cunt grip the head of my cock. I start kissing up the column of her neck and she breaths, "More. Please!" I push a little more of my length in and out slowly. Edin pants as I pull the shoulders of her dress down, exposing her breasts. Her pink nipples are hard with arousal. I let out a low growl and plunge deep into her. Pumping hard, I take her nipple into my mouth, pulling and teasing while she greedily grabs at my back and hips, wanting me deeper. I lean into her ear, "Will you cum for me, Little Hellion?"

"Yes!" she moans, as her pussy clenches around my cock.

Edin's eyes roll back as she rides out her orgasm. I continue thrusting into her, the sound of our bodies slapping together almost sends me over the edge. Her moans become louder, and her pussy tightens, telling me she is close to climaxing again. She arches her back, being taken over by another wave of pleasure, and I can no longer contain myself. My wings extend out as I grab her body, pulling her towards me, and driving deeper as my orgasm rips through me. I lean over her, kiss her chest, and whisper, "You are so beautiful, Edin." She is breathless and barely opens her eyes as she gives me a satisfied grin.

CHAPTER 25

EDIN

Through the post-orgasm fog, I feel Osiris lift me up and carry me out of the library, through the castle. We make our way up the stairs, and I wrap my arms a little tighter around his neck.

"Do not worry, Little Hellion, I got you," Osiris chuckles.

"I know," I giggle, nuzzling my nose into his neck. His scent of teakwood and sea salt makes my eyes roll back. Images of my fated mate mark flash through my head. I push the thought aside, as I have decided I no longer care. My fate has been forced upon me in every other aspect of my life, my love life will not be a part of it. I will choose my own mate, on my own time. *Although I would not mind the view of Osiris for all eternity.* I snicker at the thought.

"What is so funny?" Osiris asks, raising an eyebrow.

"Oh, nothing," I smile.

He tilts his head down, kissing me on the forehead. Osiris lays me down in bed and pulls the covers up over me, tucking me in. His body makes a dip in the mattress as he slides in next to me. He wraps his arm around me, and his wing falls over our bodies. I can barely keep my eyes open as his soft breathing lulls me off to sleep.

CHAPTER 26

ENDRICKS

Stepping through the veil to Purgatory, I walk through the long ever-changing labyrinth of hallways until I see an old door on rusted hinges with sunlight shining through the rotting wood. I stand at the foot of Gehenna Castle. Ascending the long stone steps to the castle gates, I nod to the guards standing post as they allow me entrance. It is barely dawn here, but I am not in any mood to waste time. I enter the castle and make my way to what, I assume, is the quarters of the new goddess. Walking through the doors without a knock, I am slightly taken aback at what I see before me. "Well, it seems you have made yourself quite at home, have you not, Your Highness?" I take a moment to stare at a bare-chested Edin curled up to an Elysian soldier, assuming from the gold-gilded armor strewn about. I bring my eyes back up to her face, noticing her pointed ears. *Nephilim.* "Did not realize this was a part of your training. Is this the new welcoming each individual receives upon entering Purgatory?" I chuckle, finally waking her.

Her eyes stretch wide, as she attempts to cover her naked body. "Who the hell are you and why are you in my bed chambers?!" Edin yells, throwing an empty wine glass towards my face, and missing horribly.

Stepping over the broken glass, I chuckle, "We will work on your aim first because that was just pitiful."

Clenching her fist tight against the silk blankets that she still has tightly pulled to her chest, Edin yells, "I will not ask again, who the hell are you?"

I give her a smug look, "My apologies, I am your concierge service, here to get your morning tea order, Your Highness." Edin keeps a flat face, clearly not appreciating my humor. I continue, "I am here for your training, which starts today, right now. Get up, get dressed, and possibly shower first, you reek of sex. Meet me in the courtyard for your first lesson." Leaving no room for a response, I walk out, closing the door behind me.

CHAPTER 27

EDIN

I stumble out of bed while attempting not to wake the sleeping Osiris next to me. I am not sure why I am concerned, since he did not even stir during the invasion five minutes ago. "The nerve," I mutter to myself, dropping my blanket and stepping into the shower. Osiris did mention I would have training, but what he left out was that a man dressed head to toe in black leather would come bursting into my bed chambers on the first day. Finishing up in the shower, I take a moment to look over my newly obtained tattoos: the crest of the goddess on my chest and my apparent fated mate mark on the back of my shoulder. *Could Osiris really be my fated mate?* Pushing all my thoughts aside, I neatly plait my hair and pull on my pants, tunic, and boots. I take one last glance at the slumbering Osiris in my bed before heading down to the courtyard.

The sun is finally rising as I step into the courtyard, the morning fog still standing. I spot the man who rudely woke me up just thirty minutes prior. He is fully dressed in black leather, with a fitted jacket. Straps run across both thighs, holding rows of daggers. I stomp straight over, ready to interrogate him, as he cuts me off.

"You are late," he says dryly.

"How can one be late for something they were not even aware of?" I knew that my training was in order, just not in this manner. I imagined it would be with an ancient-looking old man in a library where I would be drowned in knowledge.

He gives me no response as he makes his way to the far corner of the yard. "Your aim, I observed this morning, is almost humorous. We will start there," pointing to targets that line the courtyard walls. "Focus on summoning all your power into the palm of your hand and aim it at the target."

"Do I not get an introduction? I do not even know your name. Am I really to believe you are here to train me?"

Rolling his eyes at me, "Is a name really necessary for you, Your Highness? Make one up if you must."

This man is a complete asshole, and I do not even know who he is. "First, stop calling me *Your Highness*, I am not royalty, my name is Edin. Secondly, I am not sure who pissed you off already, but I know it was not me, as we were just rudely acquainted in my bedroom," I spit, clenching my hands into fists.

Walking directly up to me, stopping only a few inches from my face, he smirks, "My issue, *Edin*, is that I am here having to train you when I could be elsewhere tending to my own work. Yet, the council finds it absolutely necessary that I train a novice that is expected to be judge, jury, and executioner for all the souls of Windemere."

Shocked by his response, I grumble, "Well, I am so very sorry you are forced to be here with me, but I did not choose this either," I throw my arms up, "I did not choose any of this!" The look on his face almost makes me think he understands that I have no control over this fate, just as he has no control over his orders to train me.

Finally responding after what felt like years, he pulls the cloak back from his head and speaks, "My name is Endricks."

The red I had been seeing before begins to fade away, and for the first time I actually see the man before me. Endricks is a complete jerk, but he is strikingly handsome in the darkest of ways. I tilt my head upward just to take in his full stature. His pale skin counters his short raven black hair that falls messily over his forehead and matches the stubble across his jawline. The pointed ears and full-length black horns that curl back behind his head are indicative of a hellion. I am unsure of what his position was prior to my training, but his broad shoulders and toned physique make it fairly obvious that he is deadly. Endricks looks as if he could kill me with just a flick of his wrist, and from the harsh look in his blue eyes, he might be contemplating it.

CHAPTER 28

ENDRICKS

If only Edin knew that it was me she was so needy for just nights ago, showing me how well she could take my cock while I fucked her face. She would choke on her words if she was aware that each piercing she counted so smugly was a proclamation of my rank in Helheim. Six being the highest ranking, I am only able to gain seven when I take the throne. As thrilling as it would be to watch the smirk slide from her face at the revelation, I do not plan on exposing myself. This woman is undoubtedly breathtaking but shows to be a complete thorn in my side to train. My plans to wrap this up as quickly as possible seem to dwindle, if she plans to argue with me at every task.

I take a step back to look her over, "I expect you to be in training leathers tomorrow, a tunic and flowing pants will never do in hand-to-hand combat."

Her eyes grow large, as she says, "Combat? Why would I ever need to learn hand-to-hand combat? I am the Goddess of Purgatory."

I expected this from her, "Well, with that attitude you are easy to apprehend, but more importantly you need to be prepared for anything if you plan to rule Purgatory." Once again cutting her off before continuing this argument, I snap, "Training leathers tomorrow." Giving her my back while I point to the targets, I repeat myself, "We need to focus on the current issue at hand, your aim. Now, as I said before, focus on summoning all your power into the palm of your hand and aim it at the target.

CHAPTER 29

EDIN

Regaining my composure as I ground myself, I try to focus on the newfound magic within me. My magic feels erratic, as if it is out of touch with my soul. After years of having my mind set on a healer's life, it is quite jarring to be dealing with the dead. Pushing my thoughts aside, I will make my magic through my limbs and visualize it gathering in my palm into a bright purple orb before aiming it at the target with everything inside me. The small streak that seems to spark and fizzle out of my hand is a bit disheartening. I understand that this is all new to me, but gods, I did not expect to be this dreadfully bad.

"You are forcing the magic, it should flow through you naturally," Endricks says, stepping up behind me and molding his body against mine. "Close your eyes and picture your magic pumping through you like your veins pump your blood." He lays his hand on my chest, "Focus on your breathing."

The radiating heat on my chest where his hand lays suddenly calms me enough to focus. Widening my stance and relaxing my stiff shoulder I take one last breath in, envisioning my magic melding with my body. My power shoots from my hand with more force than the last, narrowly missing the target. Trying not to overreact at the power I conjured for the first time, I slowly step out of Endricks' grasp.

"Again," he states, not missing a beat as he points to a target further from us.

We spend the rest of the day reviewing conjuration, targeting, and proper stance. My body is screaming for a break as the sun dips behind the mountains.

"The sun is setting" I state the obvious, nodding towards the sky.

"Great observation, I will be turning in for the evening while you continue your lesson," Endricks grabs his things as he speaks.

"You really do not expect me to continue alone after training all day, do you?"

Without saying a word, Endricks leaves the courtyard snapping his fingers. I watch as ice spindles erupt from the ground lining the yard, intertwining with itself creating an enclosure, confining me to the training area. Running to the edge of my newly acquired, frozen cage I begin pushing against the bars. A burning sensation immediately runs up my fingertips. "Shit! What is this?!"

My hands turn a shade of blue with impending frostbite. "Of course, enchanted ice," I hiss. Knowing my attempts will be fruitless, I give up and continue training.

My magic has a mind of its own. One attempt, I am able to hit the furthest target, and the next, I am left on my ass from it backfiring. I can feel it align within me and then almost tear itself apart like it is being rejected. Many hours pass by practicing before I can no longer stand from exhaustion. Slumping over against the stone wall, still in disbelief that I am locked outside in my own courtyard by some man who just waltzed in today, my eyes slowly close.

CHAPTER 30

EDIN

I wake up on the cold ground to the sun rising over Gehenna Castle. Attempting to stretch my sore limbs, I mumble to myself, "Asshole." I turn, hearing the sound of the ice abruptly melting away in a wave of water, soaking the ground as Endricks walks through.

"Did I hear you call for me?" He stands, grinning at me.

Turning away from him, in no mood for his games, I slowly get to my feet, swiping at the dirt on my tunic to no avail. I am filthy. "How dare you leave me out here all night! You are well aware that hellhounds live in these forests," I wince, leaning my sore body against the stone wall.

I am immediately met with Endricks too close for comfort, hands pressed against the stone on each side of my head, the scent of smoke and cedarwood filling the air. "You know I am the scariest thing in this realm," he bites.

In any other case, I may have enjoyed being put in this position, but this man is a tyrant who left me to sleep outside like an animal. Refusing to play into his games, I slam both my hands into his chest in an effort to push him away, but the man is solid. I stand there challenging him while the same calming heat I felt the day before begins seeping into my palms where we touch. "I need to shower Endricks," I grunt, "Unlike you, I did not sleep in a clean bed. Now that I am thinking about it, where did you sleep?" I raise my eyebrows at him.

"In the guest quarters. of course. I am not a barbarian here to take over your castle, Your Highness," he says, finally releasing me.

"I am going to shower, change, and eat. Then I will return," I yell over my shoulder. I quickly leave the courtyard, giving him no time to respond as he so often does to me.

CHAPTER 31

EDIN

Opening the doors to my bed chambers, my eyes immediately land on the single tulip and envelope on my bedside table. I rush over and break open the wax seal. Bringing the tulip to my nose, as I read over the letter.

My dearest Little Hellion,

I apologize for leaving in such a hurry. I have received orders to promptly return to Elysia to handle an urgent matter. I hope your first day of training has gone well, and I look forward to hearing about it. I will return as soon as possible.

With love, Osiris

"He remembered," I whisper to myself. If only Osiris knew how much better, his letter makes me feel after the hellish night Endricks just put me through. I bring the tulip back to my nose before heading towards the washroom. I opt to draw a bath instead of a shower to soothe my aching limbs. Late to training, or not, Endricks will be a tyrant. I have never been so thankful for my mother and her herbology lessons more than now, as I toss dead sea salt and devil's claw into the basin. I sink low into the tub, finally having a moment to collect my thoughts over the past few days.

Why does Endricks seem to have it out for me? I can understand him not wanting to be here, but he does not have to be a complete asshat. Also, what in Helheim is wrong with me for finding him so attractive? His eyes though, look just like the masked man's from the Enlightenment. I miss Blackburn and Blythe. Would I be able to travel home once I am able to open the veil? Could they visit here without dying? And where did all the souls in the village go?

Pulling myself from thoughts before they consume me, I force my way out of the soothing water and prepare myself for another day of torture.

Can I die if I am already in Purgatory? That would be ironic.

CHAPTER 32

ENDRICKS

She is late, again. Edin truly plans to make this as intolerable as possible. I have been waiting in the courtyard for every bit of two hours. Tired of waiting, I make my way up the castle steps to drag her from whatever is hindering her. Heading directly to my quarters last night I did not notice the open balcony doors that lead to the library with what seems to be an entire fortress made of books. Taking a moment, since she is in no hurry, I walk into the library. Stacks and stacks of books lay around the fireplace with a blanket and a half-empty cup of tea, "Eager to learn, but not from me I see." Edin must have been in here prior to my arrival as I have given her no time of her own since. Grabbing the open book closest to the blanket, I read the title, *"History of Fated Mates."* I can not help but chuckle, "The Goddess is looking for love." The sound of footsteps descending the stairs lets me know Edin has finally decided to make her appearance. I set the book back in the position I found it and slip out of the library through iron and glass doors that connect to the courtyard.

CHAPTER 33

EDIN

I walk out of my room with the decision made that if Endricks wants to fight, I will show him a fight. Today's training would be hand-to-hand combat, and growing up with five older brothers is about to come in handy. He looks as if he has not moved from the spot I left him, but that was hours ago. *Did he really stand here the entire time? I would not be surprised, the man is insane.* Dressed in my new training leathers, I am feeling just as bare as I did at the Enlightenment. The leather hugs every curve of my body so tightly. Making my way over to Endricks, cutting him off before he can even say a word, I huff, "I know, I am late."

Unamused with my words, he removes all the daggers from his vest and pants. "Just get into a fighting stance and we can begin there," he says, waving me away.

Acting as though I had no idea where to begin, I stand with my legs together, knees straight, and fist at my chest. I may have five brothers who taught me how to fight, but I will need the upper hand to take Endricks down. Almost immediately Endricks begins criticizing my stance. He kicks at my boots to spread my legs apart and grabs my wrist, jerking my fist up toward my face.

"Eyes on me," he nods.

I lock eyes with Endricks, stunned by the urgent throbbing between my legs that his grasp does to my body. I pull my eyes away and stomp the degrading thoughts out of my mind. I steady myself in the position.

"Ready?" Endricks smirks, raising an eyebrow.

"Ready," I grunt.

Swiftly, I swing my leg up and around using our height difference to my advantage, taking his feet out from under him. I cross my arms, as I stare down at him with a smirk on my face. Although the sound his body makes as it hits the ground brings me great joy, it is short-lived after seeing the petrifying look on Endricks' face.

"Cunning, are we? Let us see you do it again," he grumbles, picking himself up.

I step back into position ready to fight for my life.

CHAPTER 34

ENDRICKS

Irritation crawls through me that Edin has so craftily taken me down, but I am also surprised at how well she did it. Brushing my hair back through my fingers, I step back into position. I wait for her to make the first blow, beginning to circle her. I watch as she brings her leg up again, attempting to kick me in the chest. I grab her by the ankle and send her straight to the ground. I squat to the ground with a smile, "Again."

Back in position I make the first move, catching her off guard using the same silly little move she did on me. Back on the ground she goes, with a thud. I plan to go easier on her this round, to actually teach her, but the anger across her face is quite amusing.

"Again," she grumbles, readying herself.

Edin makes the first move slamming her fist into my ribs. I reach for her, but she leans low, swiveling her hips, landing another kick to my chest. I block her next swing, throwing her off balance. Edin attempts to redirect with her other fist, but her body collides with mine, sending us both to the ground.

CHAPTER 35

EDIN

I hit my face so hard on the way down I did not remember where I was for a moment. I push my silver strands of hair back off my face. Gathering myself, I realize I have landed on top of Endricks. Sheer panic runs through my body as I scramble to get off of him.

"Stop," he says, running his thumb across my bottom lip. I stare down at Endricks, my hands still on his chest. "You are bleeding."

I do not feel the pain from the adrenaline rushing through me, only the familiar heat that radiates from where our bodies touch. "It is fine! Just a scratch," I stutter, pulling myself up, and holding my nose as it gushes blood.

"I am not concerned, but that gash on your lip looks pretty deep."

I am not surprised by his response, ignoring him I head inside to tend to my wounds.

Finally alone, I let out a long breath as I walk into my bedchamber. The pain in my nose sets in, and I am thanking the gods for my mother's regeneration salve. I grab the jar and make my way into the lavatory. Closing the door behind me, I hear the sound of footsteps coming into my bedroom. "Gods! Do I not get a moment to myself?" I shout, swinging open the doors.

"I apologize for the intrusion, Little Hellion."

"Osiris!" He looks over my blood-covered leathers, and then up to my nose and lip.

"Who did this?" he growls, cupping my face.

"Osiris, it is okay. I am okay. I was training," I blurt out.

"Training? What brute is *training* you like this?" He questions, as anger crawls across his face. I hear another set of footsteps come down the hall.

"Lord Endricks, the brute." Endricks smirks, making his way into the bathroom. The walls feel as if they are closing in or maybe it is the building tension suffocating me.

"What a pleasure. General Osiris," Osiris growls, "Lay your hands on her again and I will cut them off."

"Is it possible she might *enjoy* my hands on her?" Endricks responds smugly.

"Enough! Both of you! This is not a pissing contest. Osiris, I tripped over my own feet during combat training. Endricks, shit, I am not even sure why you are here," I huff. Not being able to take another moment in this cramped room with them, I rub the salve on my lip and walk out, leaving the two men alone with their egos.

CHAPTER 36

ENDRICKS

Hurt her? No. The way I could use my fingers to make Edin scream out my name in pleasure is a different story, but I will not. Gods I need out of this place, this woman will be my downfall. She is the most infuriating person, arguing with me at every step. Yet the fury in her eyes when she snaps back is quite a turn-on. Osiris seems to be quite territorial of the goddess though. He has been here almost every day, which is out of character for an Elysian. Odd.

I watch as Edin stomps out of her bedroom, slamming the door behind her. "That was quite brave of you, General," I say with a smirk.

"Do not underestimate the lengths I will go for her, Endricks," Osiris snarls, leaning close into my face. "Dispel," he whispers. The room suddenly darkens, void of all sound, as the walls of the bathroom fade away. "If I truly wanted to get rid of you, I would. Though, I do enjoy the thought of leaving you here, confined to the darkest corners of your own twisted little mind," Osiris clips, flicking his wrist nonchalantly, "But I cherish Edin and support her and her training."

"Your illusions do not scare me, Osiris," I chuckle, as bands of water form around his legs, bringing him to his knees. "While you create fictional visions, I can drown you from the inside out." I squat down where he kneels, "Were you aware that half your body is made up of water?" I tilt my head as I manipulate the molecules of his lungs to swell.

Coughing, Osiris drops to his hands as his nose starts to bleed. Spitting his blood onto my boots, Osiris hisses, "Just complete her training and return to your barren hellscape!" The room slowly shifts back into view.

"I plan to," I say bluntly, as I turn and take my leave.

CHAPTER 37

OSIRIS

After cleaning myself up, making sure to look as if the dispute with Endricks never happened, I find Edin in the library surrounded by her books. "I thought you might need a cup of tea after the day you had," I say, kissing her forehead, and handing her a mug of hot tea. "I apologize again for leaving without a goodbye, I was called on urgent orders to report back to Elysia."

Edin takes the mug with both hands. "Oh," she giggles, "I assumed you lost interest in me once you got your fill and took your leave for Elysia."

Sitting down behind her, I pull her back towards my chest. "How is your training really going, my Little Hellion?" I question, rubbing her shoulders.

"I would say swell, but I would be lying," she huffs.

I lean around her and grab her chin, rubbing my thumb across her lip. "Yes, I would say so with that shiner. Do I need to go a round with Endricks?" I ask with a smirk.

"No, I am capable in combat, just clumsy," she says, leaning further into me.

"Oh, I do not doubt your capabilities at all, I could never go toe to toe with you," I tease, starting to tickle her. She tosses onto her side laughing and screaming.

Edin's laughter grows louder as I continue tickling until we are both in tears. It is in these moments she looks the most beautiful and I can truly picture a life with this woman. I stop her torture and tuck a piece of her raven hair behind her pointed ear. Leaning over her, I whisper, "How could I ever leave, when my heart lives here, my Little Hellion?"

She pushes up from the floor, locking her lips to mine, "I am growing quite fond of your company here," Edin whispers back.

"I will stay as long as you allow me," I say, pulling her even closer.

She gives me a gorgeous, yet mischievous smile. "I will keep that in mind," Edin snickers. Her mouth slowly turns downward, and her voice becomes sullen, "I truly just wish to complete my training. I feel like I am getting nowhere with it."

I roll onto my back, pulling her onto my chest. "Maybe I could be of some assistance?" I blurt out.

"How so?" she says, raising her eyebrow curiously.

"Has Endricks taken you to the veil yet?"

"No."

"Would you like me to show you?"

"Yes! Of course!" Edin squeals.

I stand up and lift her into my arms, "Then I will escort you the first chance we get, but for tonight let us get you to bed," I say, kissing her cheek as I make my way up to her chambers. I lay her in bed, pulling the covers up around her.

"Thank you for being so supportive," she yawns.

"Of course, I have no doubt you will be an astounding goddess. I must return to Elysia for a couple of days on order. I will see you soon," I say, kissing her forehead as her eyes slowly close. I can not help but stand there for a moment, taking in her beauty.

Since I laid eyes on this woman, I have believed her beauty was goddess-worthy. From her long black hair, with that one streak of silver, it is so peculiar. To her pointed ears, that wiggle when she laughs. Then to her small hands that fit so perfectly in mine. Her very touch sends a shock of electricity through me. All of that aside, after spending time with her, it is Edin herself that is a goddess. Her thoughtfulness. Her determination. Her kind heart.

CHAPTER 38

ENDRICKS

The sun has not even broken the tree line as Edin enters the courtyard. Noticing her already healing lip, I nod, "Must be pretty powerful salve you have."

"Oh," she says. Surprise runs across her face, and she covers her mouth, "My mother is a pretty amazing healer back in Blackburn." The look on her face slowly turns to sadness. "I am afraid I will never get to see her again, at least until she passes," Edin says, looking away.

"Once you are able to open the veil she may visit. You are the Goddess of Purgatory. Once your magic is in your complete control you will have the ability to allow whomever you want to come and go."

This newfound knowledge seems to bring a hope to her eyes that I am about to crush with this next lesson.

I drag a rabbit out of its cage. "Today, you will learn resurrection," I say, snapping the rabbit's neck.

Horror runs across her face, as she stutters, "What in all of Helheim is wrong with you?"

Edin drops to her knees where the rabbit lays. I knew she would react this way, but Edin needs to be pushed.

"Now use your power to bring his soul back into his body."

The disgusted look on her face quickly turns to anger. "You are a monster! I have barely learned how to control my magic and with no instruction, you take an innocent life," she yells.

Edin clearly does not understand the ramifications of the magic she wields. A necromancer holds immense power, the ability to not only commune with the dead but control the very linings of one's soul. She has been so focused on death that she forgets she commands life as well, able to reach between the veil. The woman before me could raise an entire army from the ground and who would question the Goddess of Purgatory? If only she would recognize it, and that is why she needs to be pushed.

"As a necromancer, you hold the ability to reach beyond and guide a being back. Rest your hands on his body, cast your mind out until you feel his life force, then command it back."

Edin closes her eyes and lays her shaking hands on the rabbit. A faint purple mist begins to manifest as she looks inward for his life force. The body begins to glow and rise from the ground, then it abruptly drops.

"It takes great focus to draw a life back in," I say, attempting to help but quickly being cut off.

"I am focusing, you asshole!" Edin snaps.

I watch for the next hour as the glowing mist appears, and the corpse rises and falls, before deciding that Edin has had enough for one day.

"It seems the hare is just as stubborn as you are," I joke, "We will try again."

I have become quite accustomed to death in my line of work, unbothered as I pick up the remains.

"I must go to Helheim to handle some matters. When I return, we will travel to Coemeterium," I state.

Edin gives me her back as she walks out of the courtyard. From over her shoulder, I hear Edin growl, "Just leave."

CHAPTER 39

EDIN

I feel absolutely defeated after today's lesson. I immediately strip off my clothes and step into the shower in hopes of washing the day off. I close my eyes and allow the water to run down my face letting my mind roam elsewhere. Needing a release, thoughts of Osiris rush in, as my clit begins to throb. Leaning back against the shower wall, my hand travels down between my thighs, and I slide a finger into myself.

My knees are pressed to my chest, feet above my ears and my head is shoved down to watch as Osiris's length pounds into me. The force of his thrust slapping against my sensitive nerves makes my eyes roll into the back of my head, gasping his name. Osiris moves his hand from the back of my head to my throat, cutting off my air as I slam my eyes shut. The sensation of floating creeps in as I tip over the edge. He releases his grip, and I take in a breath. Pleasure crashes over me as my vision comes back. I drag my eyes up his chiseled abdomen to his hard chest. Confusion hits me as intricate black tattoos appear across each pec running up his neck. My foggy vision clears to Endricks leaning over me with a smirk.

I gasp, jolted from my pervertedly corrupt fantasy. I step out of the shower, padding on wet feet across my bedroom to the massive wardrobe.

"What in the Gods is wrong with me? Endricks?!" I shiver, trying to shake the vision from my mind.

My closet here in Purgatory was already fully stocked when I arrived, with beautiful, corseted gowns and robes. *I am the Goddess of Purgatory now, I might as well dress as a Goddess*. I shrug, grabbing a black sheer robe with a long flowing train. I have not been alone in Gehenna Castle for more than a day's time since I arrived and the silence is quite nice. Walking the long halls, I make my way to the library with a cup of tea in hand. The library has become my comfort. The stained-glass doors and roaring fire feel like home, calming my nerves.

I curl up on the oversized chaise with *Purgatory's Bestiary*, determined to find the black-flamed hellhound. Flipping straight to the H's, scanning the pages until I come across "Hellhound Configurations." I run my finger across the page, reading, "Hellhounds, or The Bearers of Death, were created by ancient hellions to serve as heralds of death. Known for their unusually overgrown form, supernatural strength, and accompaniment of fire. Check." I huff, continuing to scour the page, "Orange, red, and blue flames are most common, while black is a rarity, recognized for their immense power and fatality rate. A black flamed hound is usually found at the back of the pack if they belong to one at all. The reclusive hound only chooses to affiliate with beings they deem worthy of their loyalty." Laying the book over my face, I huff, "Gods."

The sun shining through the library window tells me I must have dozed off at some point. Slowly rising, I am thankful for a day off from training after the atrocious events of yesterday. I walk into the kitchen to find Sera finishing up breakfast. This woman is truly a saint.

"It smells delicious in here, Sera," I yawn.

"Well of course it does, my Dear. *I* made it and I make everything with love," Sera chirps, giving me a tap on the nose as she sets a plate down in front of me.

"I think I may take a walk through the village today," I say, stuffing my face with bread pudding.

"That would be a lovely idea, the villagers would adore seeing you. Just be careful traveling near The Deadwoods, Dear."

I quickly finish my food, and thank Sera for her kindness before going up to my bed chambers to change. Grabbing the first pair of pants and flowing tunic I see, I slip them on and then lace tight a corset over my top. I pull on my boots and grab a cloak as I head back downstairs. I nod to Darian as I pull the hood of my cloak up over my head and walk out the castle doors.

I have grown to appreciate Purgatory, it holds its own darker beauty. The landscape is reminiscent of the folklore my mother read to me as a child. I leisurely make my way down the path to the village with a basket of herbs in hand. I am aware the villagers have passed, but everyone enjoys a bundle of lavender in their bath. I hope it will be a nice show of my appreciation for their patience until my training is complete. Walking into the village, I notice it is much quieter than my last visit. I go door to door knocking without an answer.

"Where is everyone? I counted at least fifty souls here the other day."

Finally seeing someone in the distance, I head in their direction. "Hello sir, how are you today?" I smile, handing him a bundle of lavender.

"Thank you, Your Highness," the man says, bowing. His response reminds me of Endricks, and I quickly push the thought of him out of my mind.

"Do you happen to know where the rest of the villagers might be? I brought enough bundles for each of you."

"My apologies, Your Highness, but there is only me and a few others here. I assumed they had acquired their judgment."

Attempting to hide my panic, I laugh, "Of course! I must have miscounted. Thank you for your time. I hope you enjoy the lavender." I wave to him as I make my way back to Gehenna Castle.

CHAPTER 40

EDIN

I know I counted more than a few souls here the other day with Osiris. Where did they go? How vast is Purgatory? Was there another village I had not yet seen that they could have moved to? The old man thought they had received their judgment, but I am still in training. Ugh, he called me Your Highness, gross. I will never be used to that. Ugh and Endricks. I wonder what business he had to attend to in Helheim. He is a complete ass, but my day has been quite dull without him.

"Hello?"

The sound of someone calling out to me from The Deadwoods breaks me from thoughts. Is that where the villagers went?

"Hello! Where are you?" I shout, stepping to the edge of the tree line.

"We are in here," the voice calls out.

I lean further into the trees trying to see where the voice is coming from. Feeling something brush against the back of my leg, I look down to see a reptilian-like tail wrap around my ankle. Before I can think, it takes my feet out from under me. I frantically grasp at the tree roots as I am drug into the forest. Astonishingly, I am able to grab onto a stump. I wince as the bark sinks deep into my palms. I throw myself onto my back, peering up at the blood-curdling beast, trying to contain my screams. It is not quite a mortal or a hound, falling somewhere terrifyingly in the middle. Its skin hangs from its body like rotting flesh, with what I assume is its flared ribs protruding through its back. The creature has the face of a human, but it is contorted in a way that sends goosebumps across my skin.

Walking on all fours, it stands over me. A tar-like fluid drips from where its eyes should be onto my chest. I reach for the dagger at my side yet find nothing.

"Hello? I'm in here," the creature howls.

Hearing the voice, I bring my eyes back up to the beast. It twists its head around until the face is completely upside down.

The beast stares at me, as it giggles like a child, "Hello, I'm here."

I whisper a small prayer as I push my arm forward, hoping all the training I have endured will amount to something. A streak of purple shoots forth from my hand sending the creature backward, buying me a moment to get to my feet. I search frantically for my dagger, but still, nothing. I begin running in what I hope is the correct direction.

The loud crashing of branches lets me know the thing is closing in. Then the forest goes still, which is even more alarming. I begin scanning the trees, the creature nowhere in sight. A sudden wetness on my nose has me looking up, as beads of tar drip down on my face. I take off at a dead sprint in any direction other than here. The sound of the earth crumbling behind me echoes through the trees as the monster lands on the ground. The force of its landing shakes the ground and I lose my footing, slamming into a tree. Turning around and pressing my back into the bark, I prepare to fight for my life. The creature closes the gap between us immediately. Hot breath sweeps across my face as it screeches. I push my hands towards its chest, willing my magic at the beast. My power feels unstable as it pumps through me and fizzles out of my palms.

"Shit," I hiss.

Closing my eyes, I accept my fate. I will be the first Goddess of Purgatory to die in Purgatory. Thoughts of Blythe, my mother, Osiris, and even Endricks come rushing forward. At the sudden sound of chaos falling around me, I rip my eyes open. The scene before me is difficult to make out. The creature no longer has me pinned to the tree, but it is now the one pinned to the ground. A hellhound stands above it with snarling teeth and the same familiar black flame I noticed with Osiris at our last encounter. Before I am able to make sense of what I am seeing the hound lurches forward, ripping the creature's throat out. I stand, still pressed against the tree as the hound turns in my direction. He treads towards me, standing almost at my height, he meets my eyes before lying down at my feet. Taking in a breath of relief, I slowly slide down the tree, joining him on the ground.

"Thank you," I say, cautiously, reaching my hand out. "You were there when Osiris and I were attacked the other day," I smile, noticing his black flames burn brighter. He nudges his nose against my palm as I continue, "I do not know if I would have made it out of here alive if you had not shown up."

Regaining my composure, I pull myself up, slinking my way out of The Deadwoods. The light crunching of leaves behind me lets me know the hellhound is still there. He follows me all the way to the castle steps. Turning and bending down, I look at the hound.

"Thank you for escorting me home," I say, patting his head. "You know, I could use a companion around here. I think this castle is big enough for the two of us."

His ears perk up.

"I presume that is a yes," I laugh. Looking him over, his black flames remind me of a starless night sky. "I think Nyx is a fitting name for you."

CHAPTER 41

ENDRICKS

Entering back into Helheim I am met by my father, King Adonis. If he is here waiting for me at the veil, then we have an issue. My father is not the welcoming type.

"Son."

"Father."

"How are your orders in Purgatory, I assume you are still in the good graces of the Goddess?" he questions.

"Splendidly," I flatly respond.

"Do I have to remind you of the importance of your mission?" My father grumbles, giving me his back as he walks back toward his study. The halls are lined with framed portraits of every hellion to sit on the throne. "If the goddess sees you in a negative light, it could be detrimental to our numbers here in Helheim. Women are spiteful creatures and will go out of their way to ensure we feel their wrath. I would know, I was married to your mother."

Sizing up the back of his head, I snap "Do not speak about my mother or I will have your tongue."

King Adonis chuckles, not even looking back, "Ah, Endricks. My only spawn and my own personal problem."

"Why am I here father?" I growl, scanning the room as I walk into the study.

The obsidian fireplace blazes with a much too-large portrait of my father above it. A wall of ancient war weapons hangs to my left and floor-to-ceiling windows with the view of Helheim stand to my right.

Pointed obsidian skyscrapers lined in gold reach high into the dark grey clouds. The glow of fires burning off in the distance causes the streets to be filled with a never-ending haze. I watch people tread across black stone bridges over the flaming rivers. I am sure they are either heading to their daily torture sessions or delivering it, it is torture either way.

I bring my gaze back to the office. The only furniture in the room is my father's stone desk and chair. I will burn this place to the ground once I take the throne and build a new empire, allowing all the tortured memories of my childhood to go up in smoke with it. I may be my father's only heir, but he is not above murdering his own family. I watched my mother waste away under his reign for years, unable to do anything. I spent an unimaginable amount of time behind bars in Helheim prison just out of her reach. My father felt that the most efficient way to become a trained killer was to be treated as one.

Of course, he has four guards waiting in his study for us. He trusts no one. He is smart enough to not trust me. A slumped figure is strapped to a chair sitting in the middle of the room. He looks to have been here for some time from the dried blood covering his face. Jerking the man's head up by his hair, "It seems we have a traitor in our midst," King Adonis hisses.

I finally recognize the man as Zebulun, an earth sprite with time magic, and Helheim's trusted prophet. Zebulun has always been a loyal subject to the kingdom and is also the one to foretell my cursed future. His time magic is impeccably accurate, predicting the next great war or downfall of a realm, and my father uses it to his advantage.

"Zebulun has been linked to our controversy down in the prison. I have called you back to Helheim to extract more information out of him." King Adonis spits.

I drag Zebulun down into the dungeons, throwing him to the soot-covered floors. Crawling away from me, he pleads, "Please, Lord Endricks, my devotion lies with the kingdom!"

"Then why are you being accused," I snap, taking three quick strides and my boot onto his chest.

"I swear I do not know, my Lord. I have not been to the prison since I revealed your own prophecy in the cells."

Through gritted teeth, I say, "That was almost a millennium ago Zebulun!"

"Sir, I know. I am just as dumbfounded. One of the guards said I was the only person to be seen coming in or out of the prison that night."

"The same night a prisoner escaped?" I grumble, leaning more into the boot on his chest.

Barely able to speak from the pressure, Zebulun cries, "Yes, but I swear on the divine I saw no one, Lord Endricks!"

I lift my boot from his chest at the sound of cracking.

"Oh, thank you, thank you!" he stutters out between coughs.

"I never said I believed you, Zebulun," I growl, snapping my finger, and freezing his body solid where he lies. I have known Zebulun since I was a little demon and I do believe what he is saying to be true, but until I resolve

the issue it is best to keep him quiet.

CHAPTER 42

EDIN

The banging at my door can only be from one person, it lets me know Endricks has returned from Helheim. *At least he has learned to knock.* I reluctantly open the door.

"Why are you not dressed and ready to go?" Endricks questions, rolling his eyes.

Nyx immediately steps between my legs, growling at the sight of him. "Seriously Endricks, did you expect me to sit here anticipating your arrival?" The smirk on his face gives me my answer. "I will get dressed. Do I need to pack a satchel?"

"No, it should not take more than a day as long as you can keep up." Endricks points towards Nyx with a grimace, "Where did this mutt come from?"

I give him no response, slamming the door in his face.

Minutes later I am in my training leathers walking out the castle doors with Nyx at my side. Trying to keep up with Endricks, whose strides are triple my own, "What is Coemeterium?" I say between breaths.

"Coemeterium is the burial site of the gods and goddesses. It is where they are laid to rest until they choose to reincarnate."

I had not come across a book about this in the library yet. "Why do we need to go to the burial ground of the gods?"

"Cato, the last God of Purgatory, is buried with *Death's Grimoire*. It is tradition for the new God or Goddess to retrieve it themselves" he snaps, clearly agitated, "How many more questions are you going to ask me? We have a long trek through The Deadwoods, and I would like some peace and quiet."

Apparently, he did not have a warm and fuzzy welcome home in Helheim. He seems to be an even bigger ass than before.

CHAPTER 43

ENDRICKS

The Deadwoods would be no mere trek, but I would not let Edin know that. The forest is home to nightmarish creatures that even Helheim does not house. Carrows being the most deadly, a mortal-hound-like creature with the ability to mimic voices. They use this deception to lure souls into the woods to consume before a being can seek judgment from the Goddess. The forest also houses its own weather system with lethal storms, erratically changing with a thick fog that can create illusions to pull you deeper off the path. Getting Edin to Coemeterium is only half the battle and I can not help her in the next step. In tradition, the new God or Goddess must transcend into the Liminal, a space between life and death, commune with the previous God, and ask for permission to

obtain *Death's Grimoire*.

CHAPTER 44

EDIN

From what I can tell we are deep within the forest, the tall spindly trees cast shadows as we walk. I am thankful to have Nyx at my side. "Are we almost there? It is getting harder to see with this mist."

"Yes, Your Highness, not much further," Endricks growls.

I swear if he continues to call me that I will let Nyx rip his throat out. *How can one be so attractive, yet completely unbearable?* Another hour goes by when the trees finally part, creating a massive circle with obsidian pillars lining the perimeter. A waterfall that seems to flow straight out of the heavens sits in the middle, with hundreds of statue-like headstones lined around it, creating a spiral. I stop for a moment to take in the beautiful scenery that is truly fit for a god's rest.

"Let's go, Lady," Endricks yells from across the bridge, pulling me from the trance.

Looking over the edge as I cross, the trench below is so deep I can not see the bottom.

"Some say you can reach Helheim through the trench," he nods, kicking a stone down into the dark abyss. "While others say if you are able to rise up the waterfall, you will reach Elysia."

Walking around I read each name on the headstones. I was not aware there were so many gods. I finally come to Cato's headstone, "Now what?"

"You must do this part alone. Thrust your soul into the Liminal and ask his permission for the tome."

"Liminal?" I stare at him.

"The Liminal," Endricks huffs, "The spiritual realm between life and death for the Gods."

"Oh…"

He makes it sound so easy. I stand there for a moment to calm my racing heart and give myself an inner pep talk. *You are the Goddess of Purgatory. You are capable!* Grounding myself, I push my mind beyond, reaching out even further than the gray areas of Purgatory. I wander through the Liminal for what feels like centuries calling out to Cato when the space below me seems to give out. Bracing for impact, I pry open my eyes to the realization that I am floating. Standing before me is Cato. I expected a giant from my memories of him at the Enlightenment, but he is the exact opposite. Cato stands at about half my height, a frail, but wise-looking old man.

"I have been expecting you, Edin of Blackburn," he says, waving me forward.

"I have come for your blessing to obtain *Death's Grimoire*."

"Do you understand the great power you hold? The immense strength it must take to wield the true power of Purgatory? The strict morals you must uphold and also hold yourself to?"

"I do," I nod, standing straight.

"I hope you do," he says, touching his index finger to my forehead.

The space around me begins to shift as the familiar smell of eucalyptus and lavender takes over. I am home, back in Blackburn, standing before my parents' apothecary with *Death's Grimoire* in hand.

Oh, thank the divine gods, it is over.

Rushing inside to see my mother prepping tonics. I throw my arms around her neck. "I missed all of you so much," I cry, as her warm embrace settles my nerves.

"My sweet girl, we have missed you. We are so very proud of you and your accomplishments. Will you be able to stay or must you return to Purgatory?" she questions, with a hopeful look in her eyes.

"I do not think I can stay mother, but I was told I would be able to visit."

I plan to make the best of what time I have, as I am unsure of how long that will actually be. I spend the rest of the evening jarring salves and tonics as I did before my new title, telling my mother all about Purgatory.

The breaking of glass sends me into a panic as I turn to see the flickering of a fire catch outside the window. The flowers that hang from the sill immediately go up in flames. The room begins to be consumed by the fire as I pull my mother out the door, throwing our bodies to the ground coughing.

"What in all of Helheim is going on?" I say, watching my childhood home go up in flames.

"Crone! Crone! Crone!" is being chanted and getting louder by the second as a mass of villagers turn the corner of the burning building. I watch in confusion as my mother is wrenched from my arms and handcuffed.

"Odessa, you are charged with murder by poison!" Merlin, an older prophet of the village, bellows through the growing crowd.

Reaching for my mother to pull her back, "This is preposterous, my mother has been a loyal healer to the village for over a millennium!"

"The death of three good samaritans has been traced back to your mother's tonic, Edin."

The look on my mother's face is blank as they tie her to a tree. The villagers wheel out the remains of the dead as proof, dropping them at my feet.

Finally looking at me with watery eyes, my mother cries, "My sweet girl, you know this is wrong. You are a goddess, make them understand!"

Patting my shoulder and placing a torch in my hand, Merlin speaks, "Yes Edin, as goddess your word is final."

"My mother is a saint! As I said, she has been nothing but a loyal healer to the village, tending to all your ailing needs! How dare you disrespect her with these accusations!"

My thoughts are abruptly pulled back to earlier in the apothecary as I watched her inject the tonics with a deep gray liquid. Sagebrush, a crucial element to the tonic's healing abilities, the scent it gave off was different than I remembered, but I was unable to put my finger on it. My stomach drops, as bile runs up my throat.

"Mother, how could you?" I grind out.

A shiver runs up my spine, knowing now that it was poison hemlock. The pain in my chest intensifies as I realize what I must do. With tears in my eyes, I kiss her forehead, saying a silent prayer to the gods for her mercy. I fall to my knees, the pain too much to bear.

"Forgive me, Mother," I whisper, dropping the torch at her feet.

Still, on the ground, I wipe the tears from my swollen red eyes. I realize I am no longer in Blackburn, but kneeling before Cato.

"Very good, Edin," he says proudly, "As the newest Goddess of Purgatory you will be faced with excruciating decisions to make. You must never be swayed by empathy or your emotions. Your loyalty shall not waver from what is just in this cruel realm. Good luck, my child." Cato begins to fade away, and *Death's Grimoire* manifests before me.

"Wait! I have so many questions," I choke out, still shaken from my trial.

"Everything you need is within the book," his words are barely a whisper before he vanishes, leaving me in the dark.

I begin wandering through the foggy space attempting to feel the tether to my body. Trying to calm my still-shaking hands from the traumatic event, I faintly hear my name being called in the distance. The Liminal seems never-ending as I walk, the shouting of my name no closer or further away than before. No matter what direction I look it is all the same misty black depth, reminiscent of the night sky.

Had I been walking for minutes or hours? Time seems inconsequential here.

CHAPTER 45

ENDRICKS

Why does this woman have to drag out everything?
It was a very simple task, go to the Liminal, ask the bag of
bones for the book, and get back.

I have been in a staring contest with this mutt for well over an hour now, and the thing looks like it wants to rip my face off. I finally look away to check on Edin's body sprawled out on the ground where she landed. *I guess I could have caught her.*

Noticing her fingers and hands have become translucent, I huff, "Shit, she can not find her way out." I immediately begin to shake her as I call out her name. "Edin!" I stop myself, realizing I am shaking her to the point it may hurt her. Taking a deep breath, I attempt to stay calm and in control of the situation, but the engulfing pain in my chest will not allow it. I have been yelling for over ten minutes now to no avail and the translucency is traveling quickly up her arms.

Straddling her I grab her face, yelling, "Edin! You are too stubborn to end like this. Feel for your tether, damn it!"

Nyx cries out with a chilling howl and nudges her face.

Running to the waterfall, I begin dumping water over her face attempting to shock her body, but my efforts are fruitless. The fear of losing her in the Liminal sends me to my knees. I jerk her limp body close to my chest, begging, "Damn it, Edin! Please!" Losing any control I have left, I crush my lips against hers.

CHAPTER 46

EDIN

The yelling of my name seems to be getting louder as the pressure in my chest builds. I look down at *Death's Grimoire*, noticing my hands have become translucent. Panic runs through me as I strain my ears listening for my name. The pressure in my chest feels as if I am suffocating. I gasp for air as the world around me begins to shake. I spin around searching for anything in this black abyss of a realm. Suddenly, streaks of purple shoot out from the depths, like a lightning storm, and I feel the familiar tug of my tether. The translucency has crawled up my arms as I take off running towards the building purple storm. I can now hear my name being yelled as I spot my tether back to Coemeterium. Seizing the cord, a sharp shooting pain sets my body alight as purple electrical streaks creep up my arms.

Gasping for air, I feel like I have been drowning, and from my water-logged clothes, I might have been. I open my eyes to see a distressed-looking Endricks, way too close to my face. Pushing him off me, I cough out, "Did you try to fucking drown me?" H

He scoffs, "I think what you are trying to say is, thank you for saving my life." The concern completely disappears from his face.

"I had it under control, *thank you*."

"Oh, yes for sure. Your body was just fading into the Liminal."

I slowly sit up, pulling *Death's Grimoire* to my chest, as Nyx comes to sit with me. Petting him while he bares his teeth at Endricks, I smirk, "You would never let anything happen to me, would you boy?"

"Once again, where did this mutt come from?" Endricks grumbles, throwing his hand towards Nyx.

"The Deadwoods."

"Come again?" The tone in his voice becomes more stern. "I did not stutter. The Deadwoods, Endricks."

"You went into the Deadwoods alone, and made it out alive?"

I roll my eyes, "Well I am here to tell the tale, am I not?" I would not dare tell him about the beast I encountered or how Nyx saved my life. I am just thankful we have not seen one since.

"It seems I have underestimated you, Your Highness," Endricks says, taking a bow. The sarcasm in his voice tells me he does not believe a word I am saying.

"Can we please get out of here? I am soaking wet, thanks to you and it is getting colder by the minute."

"As you wish, Your Highness."

I am certain of one thing at this point, the man only has two moods: sarcastic jerk and indignant asshole.

CHAPTER 47

ENDRICKS

I did not expect it to take this long at Coemeterium and the sun is beginning to set quickly. The Deadwoods would be even harder to navigate at night. I shove Edin's shoulder, "You want to lead the way? Since this is apparently your fighting ground."

She gives me no response as she heads over the bridge back into the cover of the forest. I pull two torches from my satchel, dragging the flint tip across a headstone to light them.

"What kept you in the Liminal?"

"I would rather not talk about it," she responds curtly.

Keeping to myself, I scan the trees for anything lurking in the shadows as we leave Coemeterium. We have been walking in silence for well over an hour and the sun has completely set, our only light source being the moon and our torches.

"I can not see a damn thing through this fog," Edin whines, swatting in front of her face.

"Just stay on the path and we will be fine. Anyways, you will protect us. Will you not?" I laugh, tapping her back.

"Is sarcasm your only language? I was in The Deadwoods once and not by choice."

"Did someone force you into the woods?" My tone comes off as more protective than I intended.

"Not exactly, I went to the village and most of the villagers were missing. On my way back to the castle I heard someone calling to me from the trees and I thought it was possibly them."

"You never listen to the voices that call out to you from the Deadwoods," I say, shaking my head.

"I thought I heard my villagers."

"What you heard was a carrow, I am surprised you are alive."

"A carrow?" Edin questions.

"Yes, a carrow, a creature native to Purgatory, that feeds on souls."

Her silence tells me that is exactly what she ran into. The spindly tree branches begin to sway as the wind picks up and dark clouds seem to shroud the moon leaving us with only our torch lights.

"Stay close, these storms can be a real mind fuck."

CHAPTER 48

EDIN

Mind fuck? This entire place is a mind fuck.

Carrows? I was just forced to set my hypothetical mother

on fire and now this?

The fog begins engulfing my body, the pressure feels as if I am choking. I can barely see the black glow of Nyx's flame. Glancing over my shoulder I can no longer see Endricks. "Endricks, is this normal?"

"Yes, like I said, just stay on the path."

It looks as though a shadow begins to pass by me, taking on the shape of a figure. A set of familiar fox ears peek through the fog.

"Blythe?" I call out.

"It is not real, Edin," I faintly hear Endricks say.

"Edin, thank the Gods, I found you. These woods are dangerous."

"Blythe! How did you get out here?"

"Never underestimate your best friend," Blythe laughs, giving me a wink. "Come on, let's get you back on the right path. This fog can really be a mind fuck."

"That is what Endricks said," I respond, as Blythe loops her arm in mine.

The fog has become so thick I can no longer see even a flicker of Nyx's flame as we walk down the path. As the wind begins to howl, the sound of branches snapping fall all around us as we walk. Goosebumps crawl across my skin.

"Blythe, how did you find me?"

Another gust of wind spreads through the trees, taking the flame of my torch with it. I grip onto Blythe's arm tighter as we stand in the dark, but I can no longer feel her fingers intertwined in my own. Her arm that I had been holding fades into a mist.

"BLYTHE?" The fog suddenly settles and my vision adjusts. Trees surround me with no path in sight. "BLYTHE? NYX? ENDRICKS? Shit," I yell. "Endricks could have been a little clearer about the woods," I grumble, "mind fuck."

I search through the trees for the glow of Nyx or Endrick's torch, but all I can see is an endless forest through the darkness. "I took maybe three steps with Blythe or whatever that thing was. How did I get *this* far off course?" I look to the sky hoping for any indication that I am walking in the right direction. Something grabs onto my shoulder. My mind immediately goes back to the carrow as I grab my dagger and send it deep into its body behind me.

Once again, I am shoved into a tree, unable to catch my breath from the force of it when I hear, "Seriously?"

Tilting my head back I am met with the blue eyes of Endricks, "Oh thank the Gods it is you!"

"Thank the Gods? You just fucking stabbed me in the shoulder."

I spin around to face him. "Well, I am sorry I thought you were a carrow. Do not go grabbing people in the woods and that will not happen," I say with a smirk.

"Okay, next time I will let you fall in the trench," he says, grabbing my neck and twisting it to look down at the gaping cavern only feet away from me. "Who walks while looking at the sky?" He grumbles.

"You really could have explained the dangers of the Deadwoods better."

"Would you really have listened?" he asks, tilting his head. "Now stay at my side, we will follow the cavern until we get back on the path," Endricks grinds out, as I pull my dagger from his shoulder.

CHAPTER 49

ENDRICKS

This woman will truly be the death of me. We are

barely past the tree line of The Deadwoods and she is

following her inanimate friend off into the woods. I am a

trained killer, an assassin for the King of Helheim. Yet, I

am tasked with fucking babysitting her. She needs a leash.

We continue following the cavern's edge, the path

nowhere in sight. Through the trees, I can see a clearing

coming up ahead.

"Oh, gods! Finally!" Edin huffs, as she takes off

running for the opening.

"Wait! Gods," I shout, watching Nyx take off

behind her. I push through the branches to see Edin

standing in the clearing with an abandoned building. She spins around towards me.

"This is not the village near Gehenna Castle. Where are we, Endricks?"

"Looks like the outskirts of Purgatory," I nod to the collapsing house, "And that is your castle for the night."

"What? Why?"

"Well, it is midnight and I am not dragging your ass back through the forest in the dead of night."

I slam my shoulder into the jammed door of the house, splinters of wood flying as it opens. I step to the side allowing her to walk in first.

"You have got to be kidding me?" Edin groans.

"Not to your liking, Your Highness? Maybe next time we will stay on the path."

"No, the problem is there is only one bed in this place," she snaps, throwing her hand towards the corner, where a small bed and a thin blanket sit.

"You take the bed. I am fine," I say, crossing my arms.

"You are the one that was stabbed, you should probably rest," she smirks, raising an eyebrow at me.

"I said I am fine."

"Perfect, so am I." she huffs, mimicking me by crossing her arms.

"You are the most infuriating being. Do you have to argue with me at every task?"

"Yes," Edin laughs.

I rub my temples, "Why?"

She drops her arms, balling her hands into fists, "You have been a complete ass to me since the day you walked through the veil. Can we not just both rest?" Edin swings her hands towards the bed.

"Absolutely not," I snap.

"And why not? You have an issue?" She raises an eyebrow at me.

"Gods! Fine. Take your leathers off, you are still wet from Coemeterium."

"Okay and wear what, Endricks?"

I slip off my outer jacket, pulling my shirt over my head. "Here" tossing it to her as I button my jacket back. I turn my back as she undresses and slips into my shirt.

I watch Nyx circle in front of the door before finally lying down. The squeaking of the bed springs lets me know she is decent again. I slowly turn to find her crawling across the bed. My shirt completely swallows her but rides up just enough to see the curve of her ass as she makes her way to the far corner. Sitting down on the edge of the bed, which leans under my weight, I lay down with her. Edin is on her side, pushed as far to the wall as possible.

"You know, you can lay down properly. You look ridiculous." She gives no response but sighs as she turns on her back the best she can in the cramped bed. The chill from her still-damp skin runs across me as our arms touch, "You are freezing."

"I am fine," she snaps, pulling her arm away.

"Why must you make everything so difficult? This is about survival, Edin," I say, pulling her to my chest. The same warmth as before rushes through me.

CHAPTER 50

EDIN

I am absolutely freezing but would not dare let him know. I would rather get hypothermia. Gods! Osiris would hate to know where I am lying, guess that will be an exciting conversation to have if we ever get out of the Deadwoods.

The heat where our bodies touch immediately washes over me. "Can not have you dying without your sweet Osiris," Endricks chuckles, "He would just love this."

"It is for survival. He will understand," I snap. "

He does not strike me as your type."

"And you would know my type? How?"

Stretching, he gives me a smirk, "That mouth of yours, you like to learn the hard way. Osiris does not seem like a man of that ferocity."

"Osiris fucks me very well if that is what you are insinuating. Also, he respects me, but none of that is your business, so drop it," I huff.

"Oh yes, I am sure your knight in shining armor is an absolute animal in the bed," he laughs.

"I am not some damsel in distress!"

Suddenly Endricks is above me with his hand wrapped around my throat, "Then prove it, because from this angle I think you enjoy being the damsel," he growls.

Silence falls around us as we stare back at one another. The heat from his grasp travels down between my legs, the sensation building into a throbbing urge. I clench my thighs to alleviate the ache.

"Hmmm?" He raises an eyebrow, his blue eyes devouring my body.

My mind goes back to my fantasy in the shower of Osiris and then somehow turning into Endricks. The desire to let him have his way with me seeps deep into my bones like my body needs it. I reach for his belt and panic sets in, realizing the position I am in. I shove Endricks off of me, coughing. He lays back down chuckling, "Goodnight, Belladonna."

"Belladonna," I growl.

"Nevermind," Endricks chuckles. Rolling away, I give him no response as my mind races.

The tension between us is always at its peak, but this...this was different. My entire body was already warm, yet when he touched me, it was as if he had set my body alight. The urge to wrap my legs around his waist and let him have his way with me...Dear gods! What is wrong with me? Endricks is the epitome of a jerk, who has shown me no kindness. Yet he constantly toys with me with his sarcastic comments. What in all of Helheim is Belladonna? Shit...Osiris. Gods, my guilt is going to consume me.

I shove the thoughts out of my mind, focusing on the lull of the crickets outside. Hearing the sound of Endricks' breathing become more shallow, I assume he has finally dozed off. With the sound of his heartbeat loud in my ear, I finally allow myself some sleep.

CHAPTER 51

ENDRICKS

The sun has barely broken through the trees as I lay next to Edin watching her rest. She has become the most annoying aspect of my life, and that is saying a lot for my line of work. However, in the calm of sleep, she is quite beautiful. Edin's raven black hair falls messily around her face. Forcing myself to go to sleep last night was excruciating. Oh, the positions I could put her body in, the way I could make her scream, make her question her own existence, but I would never allow it. I slowly ease out from under her trying not to disturb her slumber. She turns over on her stomach where I laid, letting out a snore that makes me chuckle. Edin's eyes shoot open, scanning the room until they land on me.

Wiping the drool from her cheek, my vision focuses, "Were you watching me sleep, Endricks?"

"No."

"What is so funny then?"

"You snore like a bear in the dead of winter."

"I do no such thing," she snaps, jumping to her feet as she tugs down on my shirt she is wearing.

"Oh, but you do," I say, letting the door close behind me with a thud.

The slamming of the door lets me know she is finally dressed, and I turn towards the shack. "Thanks for the shirt," she grumbles, tossing it at me and missing.

"Your aim."

"Hush."

"It is atrocious," I say, grabbing my tunic and shaking the dirt from it. "Did you not sleep well, Your Highness?" I ask, tilting my head with a smirk.

"As good as possible, in a shack, in the middle of nowhere."

"You seem...*tense*," I raise an eyebrow, "Like you are in need of a release."

"I am fine. Can we please just get back to Gehenna?"

"Can not wait to get back to your sweet Osiris?"

"Actually, yes," Edin says, crossing her arms as she walks ahead of me back into the forest.

CHAPTER 52

EDIN

I am so ready to be back at Gehenna Castle, it is finally starting to feel like home. Osiris and Nyx also help. I do miss Osiris... Gods, how am I going to explain myself after last night?

We walk in silence through The Deadwoods, even in the daylight it is hard to tell which way is correct. The tall, withered trees crowd every direction as we push through the branches.

"I assumed your mutt would have a better sense of direction," Endricks growls.

"Yes, I thought the same thing about you, being that you were the one who brought me out here." Nyx bares his teeth at Endricks from my side.

"There," Endricks points, "An opening in the trees."

"Thank the Gods," I huff.

"You are welcome," he smirks, raising an eyebrow.

I grumble, "You are the most insuffer-"

"Shh!"

"Do not shh-," the faint sound of a giggling child cuts me off.

"Shit."

"Carrow?" I ask, twisting my head around.

"Carrow. Go! Get down the path and do not stop no matter what you hear."

The child-like laughter grows louder as branches snap to our left. Nyx's black flames begin to engulf his body as he growls towards the trees.

"No, I am staying."

"Seriously Edin, go! Do you always have to be so stubborn?"

I turn to yell back at him, and the creature comes into view, mere inches behind Endricks. "Turn around!" I yell, pulling my dagger from my vest. I launch it towards the beast. Shockingly, the blade hits its mark, sliding deep into the carrow's eye socket. Nyx lunges forward snapping at its throat while it swats, attempting to dislodge my dagger. I cross my arms, "Who's the damsel now?"

"Not the time," he grunts, reaching for his own blade. The clanging of metal against rocks has us spinning around, my dagger now on the ground. Letting out a screech, the carrow sinks low as thick tar pours from where its eye should be.

"Move!" Endricks yells, sending his dagger into the remaining socket.

The carrow moves quicker than my mind could comprehend, suddenly pouncing forward and slashing at my face. Stumbling, I grab my cheek, blood begins to drip down my chin. I hit the dirt, landing on my ass. The monster stalks towards me as I crawl backward trying to avoid another hit. Nyx locks eyes with me, I watch them turn completely black, his entire body alight. Leaping onto the carrow's back, he sinks his teeth deep into the carrow's shoulder, ripping at its skin. The creature wraps its tail around Nyx's body, squeezing him, the sound of his ribs cracking sends me into a panicked rage. I quickly push to my feet as I watch Nyx slam into a tree trunk with a yelp. His body goes limp on the ground as it stalks up to him for a second blow.

I throw my hand up. "STOP!" I scream, my voice breaking from a mixture of anger and fear.

The beast halts, slowly turning its gaze to me. Shaking with rage, I peer up at the carrow, readying my second blade. Where black tar had oozed before is now a purple mist flowing from its eyeless stare. Meeting me directly, the carrow stands at attention, never moving. I can not make sense of the situation. The familiar frost of Endricks' magic crawls up the carrow's body, and the skin begins to shatter like glass, before completely imploding into icy shards. Endricks appears through the icy mist that was once the carrow, "You good?" he nods.

My eyes go back to Nyx who is still slumped on the ground, and I take off running. "NYX!" Tears well up in my eyes as I fall to my knees in front of him. "Nyx, please!" I cry, rubbing his now smoldering skin. His eyes sluggishly open as he nudges my hand with his nose, taking his last breath.

"Edin," Endricks whispers, laying a hand on my shoulder.

"No!" I scream, swatting at him. I throw myself onto Nyx's body and hold him close, tears streaming down my face.

"We can not stay here, there are other carrows."

"Then go if you must!" I wail, sobbing into Nyx's neck. "Nyx, come back," I whisper, "Please come back." I lay there for what feels like an eternity holding his body. Our time together was short, but the hound had seen something within me that was enough to risk his own life for. "Thank you," I stutter out between the breaths, holding my forehead to his. Feeling his pulse again, I jolt back as his body starts to twitch. The same purple mist as before encircles us. "Nyx?" His eyes flutter open, and he slowly lifts his head, licking my cheek. "Oh Gods! You…you are okay!" I choke out, pulling him to my chest as he slowly

gets to his feet.

CHAPTER 53

ENDRICKS

She finally compelled a soul to stay within its body. Obviously, Edin just needs a little more motivation. Noted.

"It is about time you used your magic properly," I say, nodding to Nyx as he stands on his wobbly four legs.

"I am not even sure how I did it." Edin shrugs, her face still struck with astonishment.

"Sometimes you just need to be pushed to your breaking point." I holster my dagger, making my way towards the path.

"What happened back there with the carrow? It was almost as if it was put in a trance when I yelled stop," Edin asks.

"The carrow was obeying your order. They are soul eaters and you happen to be not only a necromancer, but Goddess of Purgatory. You command all the beings who reside in this realm."

"Oh," she mutters. "You should know this," I roll my eyes.

Edin does not respond, but quickens her steps, putting some distance between us. I slow my stride, stretching, my limbs sore from the fight. I watch Edin and Nyx walk side by side. The two were quite a pair, the Goddess of Purgatory and a rare hellhound. She is something all on her own, but now, with that mutt by her side, she may just be untouchable.

The path shows an opening of light with the familiar outline of Gehenna Castle off in the distance. I can finally breathe easier, knowing we have safely made it out of the Deadwoods. *Barely*. I slow my pace to almost a stop as I watch Edin take off running after a red-haired figure standing at the foot of the stairs of Gehenna Castle.

"Osiris!" she squeals, throwing herself into his arms.

"Well hello, my Little Hellion," Osiris bellows as he picks her up, swinging her around.

As Osiris turns back around, his eyes land on me and then Nyx, all the warmth from before suddenly gone as he sets Edin back on her feet. "Endricks," he grimaces.

"Osiris," I nod.

I watch him wrap an arm around Edin, pulling her close. "I appreciate you accompanying the Goddess on her journey to Coemeterium, but your assistance will not be needed tomorrow, as she will need her rest," he says with a smirk.

"Understandably so," I nod, taking my leave before my irritation shows.

CHAPTER 54

OSIRIS

I watch the massive black flamed hound never take his eyes off Edin, following her every move. "Come, my Little Hellion, we need to get you some food and a bath," I say, swooping Edin up into my arms, "Then I want to hear all about your endeavors." The same electrical current runs through me as I bring her close, carrying her through the entrance of Gehenna Castle. Her slight look of concern tells me I am in for a tale. Sitting her down on the kitchen counter, I begin setting out ingredients for a meal.

"You are cooking?" she giggles.

"I am," I smile, raising an eyebrow.

"Where is Sera?"

279

"I gave her the night off, I hope you do not mind. I just want to take care of you for the night," I say, leaning in for a kiss.

She wraps her arms and legs around me. "I would love that, but let me help," she says, as her lips meet mine.

"And what would you like to be in charge of?" I laugh, happy to oblige.

"I will make the best honey biscuits you have ever had," she giggles and playfully pokes my nose.

I pull her to the edge of the counter for another kiss. "I would love that."

CHAPTER 55

EDIN

Nyx lays down at my feet, taking up half the kitchen floor, while I knead the dough for the biscuits. "I missed you," I say, smiling at Osirus.

His stormy grey eyes light up, and returning the smile, he responds, "I missed you as well, Little Hellion."

My stomach fills with butterflies as we stand in the kitchen, side by side, cooking dinner together.

Osiris nods towards Nyx, "Is this the same hound from the village? He looks quite familiar."

"Yes, he has become my sweet companion and does not leave my side."

Nyx perks up, lazily beating his flaming tail against the floor, as if he understands that I am talking about him. I cut the biscuits and lay them neatly on the pan. "The past few days have been draining," I groan, taking a sip of the wine that Osiris poured us before starting dinner. *That is an understatement.* "We traveled through the Deadwoods to the graveyard of the gods."

"Coemeterium," Osiris states.

"Yes, I had to send my soul into the Liminal and get a book called..."

"*Death's Grimoire,*" he finishes my sentence.

"Exactly," I smile at him, poking the spoon I used to stir the honey butter toward him. "Well, then I became trapped for what seemed like years in the dismal space trying to find the tether back to my body. When I finally surfaced back in Cometerium, I was drenched in water. Endricks was hovering over me claiming to have saved my life."

"Meaning you almost did not make it back to your body?" Osiris stops cutting onions and looks over at me with his brow furrowed.

In an effort to lighten the severity of my statement, I say, "I think Endricks was just being dramatic, he tends to over-exaggerate, especially when it makes him look good."

Osiris leaves his cutting board and comes up behind me, wrapping his big arms around my shoulders. His warmth melts my taut muscles, calming my nerves. "I am glad you are safe," he says, kissing my head. Osiris releases me and goes back to making dinner. "Tell me the rest, how was the trip back through the Deadwoods?"

"It was not uneventful, either. A storm descended onto the woods, creating some kind of apparition that looked like Blythe. The illusion almost coaxed me right off a cliff. Endricks *did* save me that time," I say, rolling my eyes, "In the process though, he startled me, and I drove my dagger into his shoulder!"

Osiris' eyes widen with surprise, "You stabbed him?"

"I thought he was a carrow trying to attack me," I shrug, grinning up at him.

"That is my Little Hellion," he beams at me with pride. "I had no doubt you would hold your own, but the fact that you stabbed him just makes it all the sweeter."

"Afterward, we had to stay in a shack for the night, there was only one bed, and we had to be close to stay warm, so you can imagine how uncomfortable *that* was."

His smile falls a bit, his happiness deflating, "I know you did what you had to do, it could not have been easy trying to sleep in such proximity to that asshole." Placing his hand on the small of my back, he guides me to the table and pulls my chair out for me. "If it were up to me, I would be here every day making sure he minds his manners, but I feel better about it knowing that *he* knows you will not hesitate to stab him," he laughs.

I carry the stack of bowls and cutting boards to the sink and wash them. "How are your orders going back in Elysia?"

Osiris breathes heavily, "Just swell. It seems they can not be a moment without me."

"I know that feeling," I laugh.

He grabs a dishcloth and starts drying the clean dishes. "I would prefer not to bore you with talk of my work. I will finish cleaning up. You go relax and I will bring dinner out shortly."

"Are you sure? I do not mind helping."

He takes the wet cloth from my hand, and kisses my forehead, "Of course."

"Thank you," I smile, making my way to the dining room. I plop down in the chair, thankful to finally sit in the comfort of the castle. I rest my head back and close my eyes for a moment.

The sound of the door opening jolts me as Osiris brings the roasted chicken and vegetables to the table. "Wow, Osiris, this looks amazing. How did you learn to cook like this?" He places the biscuits and butter on the table, sitting down across from me.

"I occasionally cooked for the men in my troop. I have made quite a few bad meals and had to learn from my mistakes to finally get something decent."

"Do not be so humble, this chicken is wonderful and pairs so well with my biscuits."

"I am so glad you like it, I hope I can do it again for you sometime," he winks, filling my glass of wine again.

After a delicious dinner and two glasses of wine, I feel warm and relaxed. Osiris meets my eyes and asks, "How about a bath?"

My cheeks flush. "Will you be joining me?" I laugh, raising my eyebrows.

Osiris responds with a grin, "I want to take care of you tonight. How about I run you a bath? You can soak in the tub, and I will wash your hair for you."

My heart skips a beat. *This man is truly Elysian sent.*

We make our way up the winding staircase to my bedchamber. Osiris heads into the lavatory. I hear water filling the tub and cabinets being opened. I take the opportunity to strip out of my gown and into a black silk robe. Making my way into the other room, I see the bath is half full and bubbles are building in the deep tub.

The smells of lavender and chamomile waft up from the steam, beckoning me to enter. Osiris bows deeply, smiling up at me, just as he did the night we met when he introduced himself. Unwrapping the robe, I drop it to the floor, looking down at him. Osiris takes my hand as his eyes run up my naked body, taking in the view. Shocks run up my arm as he stares hungrily at me. I step into the bath, settle low into the hot water, and lean back. Osiris lays a rolled towel behind my neck, smoothing my hair back behind me. Taking his time, he wets my hair and pours lavender shampoo into his palm. He lathers it slowly, making sure to massage it deep into my scalp with gentle pressure. Closing my eyes, I let my tension melt away, letting go of the past few days' events, focusing on the here and now.

Osiris finishes washing my hair and moves to massage my shoulders. The circular squeezing motion of his strong hands is divine. He makes his way down my arms, working out the sore knots and making my limbs feel heavy and limp. He massages my chest just teasingly above my breasts, working his fingers deep into the tight muscles there. Feeling him move closer and closer, my nipples harden in anticipation of his touch. My breathing starts to pick up and my back arches as he lightly grazes over my breasts. A throbbing ache starts deep in my pussy, and a quiet moan works its way up my throat. He moves down my torso, running his hands slowly over the curves of my stomach and hips, teasing me to the brink of madness. His every touch leaves me breathless and wanting more.

"Please," I whimper as his knuckles skate across the top of my pelvis, so painfully close to where I want him.

He breathes in my ear, "Tell me what you want, Edin."

"You," I plead, as he takes my earlobe in his mouth and nibbles.

Osiris slides his hand down between my legs, cupping my pussy, sliding two fingers between my lips. He makes slow circles teasing my clit and kissing my neck and collarbone until I am panting. I arch my back grinding against his hand for more. Finally, he pushes a finger inside my needy pussy. I gasp, moaning his name, "Osiris."

He plunges a second finger inside me moving in and out pushing on just the right spot. My orgasm builds deep inside me, tightening my gut. I buck against his hand matching his thrust. The pulsing waves of pleasure crash over me as I slam back down into the tub still riding Osiris's hand.

Water splashes over the sides of the tub, as Osiris loses his balance, toppling headfirst in a flurry of hair and wings. I crack open my eyes to his bare feet above the water, sending me into a fit of laughter. He emerges from the water with the biggest grin I have ever seen on him. Attempting to contain myself, I clap a hand to my mouth trying to smother my laughter, but I fail miserably, and Osiris joins in howling. His shoulders shake with laughter as he wipes the water from his face and tucks his waterlogged wings behind him so he can lean back.

WHAT LIES BETWEEN

***

Osiris sits across from me in the bath, his shirt is soaked and sticking to his chiseled chest. He takes my foot in his hand and starts to rub, "I did not finish your massage yet."

My eyes meet his stare from across the tub. The heat in the room rises, and it has nothing to do with the temperature of the water. Pulling my foot from his grasp, I glide over and press my lips to his, parting them with my tongue. "I think it is time for your massage," I say against his mouth as I unlace his pants. Pulling out his cock, I grasp it with one hand as Osiris moans low in his throat. Using my other hand, I slowly glide up and down his shaft while kissing along his neck and jawline. I press my soapy breasts against his chest, feeling his heartbeat pounding against mine. His breathing becomes more rapid with each stroke. I pick up my pace, moving my hand to match his heartbeat. Grinding his teeth, Osiris throws his head back while thrusting his hips into my hand, needing more before he finishes. On my knees in front of him, I pull on his dick, forcing his hips to rise until his cock is above water. Wrapping my lips around the head, I continue the rhythm with my hand from the base to my lips, over and over again. His balls tighten, and he growls out a moan, grabbing the back of my hair and pushing himself into my mouth. I feel his cock pulsate as I take the full length of him down my throat. I slide my hand down, grasping his balls and lightly squeezing. Hollowing out my cheeks around his dick, I suck hard swallowing his cum as it hits the back of my throat. I lean up, licking a drop from my lips, and give Osiris a satisfied smile.

"Dear Gods," Osiris gasps, relaxing back into the water. "Edin, you are exquisite." He grabs my chin, pulling me in for a kiss as he lifts me to my feet. Stepping out of the water, Osiris turns back, offering his hand, and helps me out of the tub. He wraps a towel around my shoulders while kissing my forehead. "Exquisite," he whispers.

I watch Osiris shake water from his huge wings and wrap a towel around his waist. I follow suit drying my hair and wrapping a towel about my chest, tucking one end under to secure it. He makes his way to the middle of my room near the fireplace. His shoulder muscles contract as he spreads his wings and shakes them out again. The feathers shiver with his movement, they must span at least eight feet from tip to tip. Coming up behind him, I wrap my arms around his waist and lay my head in the middle of his back, just under where his wings attach to his shoulders.

"They are beautiful," I say in awe of their sheer size. "Can I touch them?" I breathe against his back. He lowers his left wing just a bit, looking over his shoulder and gives me a nod, smirking. Letting go of his waist, I run my fingers up his back and along the rows of feathers that line his right wing. His body shudders, and he rolls his shoulders, tucking his wings into his body. "Oh, I am sorry, did it hurt?" He turns to me, smiling, wrapping his arms around my waist, and pulls me into his body.

"No, it does not hurt. It just tickles a bit, like an invisible hand is trailing up my spine and across my shoulders. I am just not used to the feeling, I will get there.

Do not worry," He says, kissing me lightly. "Let us get some rest, my Little Hellion."

I smile up at him with exhaustion at the mere mention of sleep. He pulls back the covers and slides between the sheets, waving me over to lie next to him. I nestle in with my back against his chest, pulling the blanket up over me. Osiris brings his wing around, covering us both. His breathing becomes rhythmic, almost immediately lulling me off to sleep inside his protective cocoon.

CHAPTER 56

OSIRIS

Waking next to Edin, I watch her chest rise and fall next to me. *My gods, she is angelic when she is sleeping.* A bit of her raven hair has fallen across her eyes. I gently sweep it behind her ear, attempting not to wake her. She stirs slightly, just enough for me to slide my body from behind hers and roll out of bed.

Making my way down the stairs, I can already smell coffee and bacon. *Just my luck. Sera is already cooking breakfast. What a lovely woman.* Moments later, I carry a tray loaded with potatoes, eggs, bacon, fruit, coffee, and juice. Luckily, I left the bedchamber door slightly open and I quietly nudge it open with my shoulder. Edin is still sleeping peacefully, half covered in the silky black sheet.

The rise and fall of her curves bring my thoughts back to last night's endeavors and I must adjust myself. Snapping back to the present, I notice her eyes flutter open, and she smiles groggily at me.

"I smell coffee," she yawns, stretching like a cat.

I place the tray on the bed between us. I hand her a cup and flash her a grin before settling against the headboard with my own.

"What?" she asks with her eyes narrowed.

"Nothing. I was just thinking of you in the bathtub last night," I wag my eyebrows at her.

She blushes, leaning into me, "It was the best bath I have ever had. We will have to make that a weekly ritual," she wags her eyebrows back at me, making us both burst into laughter.

After breakfast we dress and ready ourselves for the day. "We are headed to see the veil today," I announce, pulling on my boots.

"I have been reading about how to harness my power and open the veil. The book says it is one of the most difficult spells to learn," she says, biting her lip.

"That is why I want to take you to see it, so you can get acquainted with the way it works. Feel its power. I am sure Endricks plans to take you soon, and I want you to get in some practice before he pulls some of his sadistic shit." I walk over to Edin, wrapping my arms around her waist, "You will learn fast and be the most powerful Goddess anyone has seen."

She looks up at me with her gorgeous smile, her pointed ears turning a bright red, "You, sir, are building me up before we even know the extent of my power but thank you."

"I feel your power when I am with you. There is no denying what dwells inside you, waiting to be released into this realm."

Edin reaches up and slides her hands against the sides of my face, lacing her fingers into my hair. "How did I get so lucky to have found you?"

"As I remember it, *I* found you," I chuckle, kissing her lips gently, and then her nose, and then her forehead.

CHAPTER 57

EDIN

I follow Osiris back downstairs and through the den, towards the back of the castle. He opens the grand set of double doors to the study, "This is the quickest way to the lower quarters of the castle, where the veil sits."

I nod, walking into the room.

At the back of the study is a bookcase. I watch as Osiris walks over to a candlestick, pulling it from its holder. The stone wall creaks as the stones shift and slide apart to a dark entrance. He lights a torch from a crate sitting right inside the entry, then reaches back for my hand. I grip his hand tightly and step into the dark.

Reaching the bottom of the stairs, the torchlight travels down the long hallway. "Stay close," Osiris says, "This part of the castle is enchanted to keep intruders out."

"What do you mean?"

"The walls are always shifting and turning, some lead to dead ends, and others…well just death."

"Noted," I grimace.

Just as Osiris had said, I watch as the hallway walls begin to shift. He runs his hand across the stone, "This way."

"How do you know?"

Osiris pulls my hand towards the stone, running my fingers across the smooth surface. My finger catches on a lip on one of the stones. Brushing my hand across it I feel the small, detailed ridges. "What is this?" I question, feeling further, but find smooth stone again.

"Justice is blind," Osiris says, "These ridges are placed on the stones to help guide us to the veil."

"That is genius," I snort.

Walking with Osiris, hand in hand, I run my fingertips across the wall, and it almost makes me forget that I am nervous about seeing the veil for the first time. The books I have read explain it as an out-of-body experience that takes practice to master. Suddenly, the stone floor begins to shake and crack. Dust plumes up all around us. I rip my hand from Osiris's grasp, taking a few steps back. Osiris leans the torch down towards the stones and I see the floor starting to separate between us.

Locking eyes with Osiris, I shout over the loud shifting of stones, "What is happening?" I look back down into a dark abyss where the floor used to be.

Osiris reaches his hand out towards me from the other side. "Take my hand, Edin. This is another part of the enchantment, just an illusion to scare you."

I glance back down to the very real cavern between us. My fear of heights sends my heart racing. Taking another step back, I stutter, "Osiris, I do not think I can."

Osiris motions with his hand, pleading, "You can, Edin. This is your fear; only you can conquer this. None of it is real." I stare down into the dark, paralyzed with fear, almost in a trance-like state. "Trust me, my Little Hellion," Osiris shouts.

I swallow the lump in my throat, and his pleas pull me from my paralysis. Taking a slow deep breath in, I hover my foot over the cavern. I reach out and feel his hand wrap around mine, as my foot meets the stone floor. My view of the dark abyss dissipates into nothing as if it was never there. Osiris pulls me to his chest, holding me tight.

"This place feeds on your fears," he says, kissing the top of my head.

We pick up our pace, continuing to follow the ridges of the stones. I hold Osiris's hand as he pulls me through the long hallways, turn after turn. Everything begins to look the same, and my mind wanders elsewhere. *It is funny how easy it is to trust Osiris, to…love him. Am I actually falling for Osiris?* He stops walking and I run into his back, bringing me out of my mental epiphany. Looking up at a massive set of doors, I realize we have finally arrived.

Just like the drawings in the books, a set of intricately carved wood doors lined in silver and blue sapphires stand before me. The doors reach all the way to the ceiling and seem to be wider than even Osiris's full wingspan. I run my hand across the blue crystals, taking in their beauty.

"Blue sapphire represents justice and perfect truth," I say, looking over to Osiris.

"That seems fitting for the Room of Revelation," he chuckles, looking up towards the ceiling.

A silver placard above the door reads *Revelation.* Osiris lifts the latch and the door swings open slowly on old rusty hinges, as if it has been closed for a century. Stepping over the threshold, torches hang on both sides of the walls are set alight, one by one, on their own. A hum of power reverberates throughout the room. The last set of torches flicker ablaze. My attention is instantly drawn to the purple haze of light emitting from the veil at the end of the long room on the pulpit. Seeming to be coming from the veil itself, a mist of fog snakes its way over the landing and down the steps, dissipating at the bottom. Everything is bathed in the enticing purple glow that beckons me to come closer. The floor drops off on the sides, leaving a pathway down the middle. Water streams past us around the edge of the walkway. I step up onto the catwalk, looking up at the flags that hang between the torches. Each flag honors a different magic. At the end of the catwalk is a grand stone staircase leading up to the veil. Holding my breath, I make my way across.

As I land on the first step, the air around me shifts. My hair flows back from my face and the skirt of my dress ripples, as if weightless. The air becomes electrically charged, and I watch the hairs on my arm rise. A buzzing feeling starts in my chest, traveling to my fingertips, and I feel the magic inside me awaken. The tangible pull from the veil is so strong that I can not take my eyes off the purple glow as I climb the steps. I find myself on the landing close enough to reach out and touch the fog billowing from the veil. I barely notice as Osiris steps up behind me, swirling the fog around my skirt. I feel his hand on the small of my back, his touch immediately comforting me. The overwhelming feeling takes over my muscles, pulling my hand toward the veil's surface

CHAPTER 58

OSIRIS

Edin lifts her hand, her magic immediately calling out to the veil, and sparks fly from her fingertips. The power that resides inside her is so strong it can barely be contained by her body. Once her mind is trained to control it, she will be an unstoppable force. Purple particles bounce off the surface of the veil as her hand hovers half an inch away. Taking a deep breath and closing her eyes, Edin leans forward. Her hand connects with the veil, creating a ripple across the surface that reverberates, turning it into a liquid-like state. Time seems to stand still as my hair lifts away from my face, defying gravity. For a moment, it feels as if we are suspended in water, drifting through the room. Seconds slowly tick by, and we do not move or speak. We stand there, just holding our breath, waiting for the veil to

open to another realm.

CHAPTER 59

EDIN

Power pours out of me into the veil. I focus my mind and will my magic toward opening a door to the realm of Elysia. My hand attaches to the surface with a magnetic force holding me in place. The veil's power envelopes us, thickening the air and slowing time. I send out tendrils of magic, searching for the connection to Elysia, reaching out as far as I can. The surface starts to pulsate and I feel my magic bounce back into my hand. I try to send it out again, forcing as much magic into the veil as I can muster. My power collides with something hard and unyielding. Sparks fly as magic is sent back into my body. Pain sears through me and I seize up, tears beginning to stream down my face. My hand is blasted from the connection with the veil, and I am sent backward, landing on my back so hard that my head slams into the stone floor. I open my eyes to a black hole of nothingness. I am falling away from reality, nothing but darkness there to catch me. I am in a world of deprivation, void of everything. I faintly hear someone yelling my name, but the ringing in my ears drowns it out. My eyelids grow heavy as a blurry figure, who I assume is Osiris, kneels over me. My limbs will no longer move. I am like a rock sinking to the bottom of a lake in the dead of night. My eyes close and I give in to the black nothingness.

CHAPTER 60

OSIRIS

I watch as Edin crumbles to the stone floor, her limbs sprawled out around her lifeless body. Fear runs through me as I drop to my knees and check for her pulse. It is faint, but still there, assuring me she is barely alive. I shake her, but there is no response. "Edin! Wake up!" I yell, watching her eyes roll into the back of her head. I pick up her limp body, carrying her in my arms down the stairs, away from the veil. I stumble over the threshold, not even realizing how quickly I got here. *Navigating the hallways back up to the upper quarters of the castle is not going to be an easy feat without a free hand.*

I toss Edin up onto my shoulder, wrapping my wing around her dangling body, freeing up a hand. I opt to walk in the dark, having no other option to hold a torch. I begin gliding my fingertips across the stone walls, feeling for the rigid stones to take me back up to the study. I try to ignore the nagging ache in my back that started when I stepped out of the Room of Revelation. I take a few more steps and hear a thud behind me, just seconds before searing pain streaks across my back.

I swing around, ready to fight whoever may be down here with us. A shock runs through me and I blink my eyes, unsure of what I am seeing. On the floor, in a ragged heap, lay my wings. My vision blurs and my muscles tremble from weakness. Fighting the feeling of passing out, I choke back the bile in my throat as I look again. My wings that had once been attached to my back now lie lifelessly on the floor, smeared in blood. Dread sinks in that something or someone must have ripped them from my body.

I jerk my head up, looking for the bastard who has done this. My body tremors from the adrenaline coursing through my veins. "Show yourself!" I roar, and it echoes down the hall. I am met with silence. My heart pounds and my breaths come in shallow, heaving gasps. I reach back, with Edin still dangling over one shoulder, and feel the bloody stumps. Pain shoots through my shoulders, and I grind my teeth through the agony as I fall to my knees.

Looking down at my bloody hand, I reach for my severed wings, but they are just far enough away that I can not reach them. I roll Edin off my shoulder as gently as I can and lay her on the floor. I need to take my wings with me and beg the gods to reattach them somehow. When I turn back to pick them up, they are even further away than before. My stomach sinks. *Have I lost my wits? Who could have done this so stealthily? I will leave my wings behind if I must, to make sure Edin is okay.*

I take a moment to breathe, calming myself. Realization hits me. *Shit! It is just an illusion.* I slowly reach back and feel for my wings, and they are right where they should be on my back. I stretch them, shaking them out just to test if they still work. *I should have known something like this would happen. I am not immune to the enchantments of the lower quarters.* Gently picking Edin up again, I sling her over my shoulder and vow not to stop again, no matter what gets in my way, until we are out of this labyrinth and I know that Edin is okay.

"Sera!" I scream, kicking open the door to the study. Gently laying Edin on the couch, I check her breathing. With each rise and fall of her chest, my panic subsides just a little. Sera rushes in, her face drawn with worry.

Her eyes land on Edin, "What has happened?" she asks.

"She touched the veil and was knocked unconscious from the power of the kickback. Bring a cold wet cloth and anything else you can think of that might help bring her around."

Sera rushes out the study doors and then returns just as quickly with a basin of cold water, some clothes, and Eucalyptus oil.

I brush Edin's hair from her face, "She was not ready. I did this," I say through gritted teeth.

Sera wrings out the cloth and hands it over to me, "For her head." I watch as she adds the scented oil to a dry cloth and holds it just under Edin's nose. Edin's eyelids flutter, but her eyes stay rolled back into her head. My heart skips a beat.

"Edin!" my voice cracks as I yell her name. I take her hand in mine, kissing the back of her palm, whispering, "Please come back to me." Despair builds in my chest as I sit, staring at her for what seems like an eternity, trying to will her back to consciousness.

"Osiris, dear, she is alive. Let's take her upstairs. Perhaps Miss Edin just needs rest and rebuild her strength," Sera says, patting my shoulder.

Begrudgingly pulling my eyes away from Edin's face, I look at Sera and her sincerity brings me a small reprieve from the panic. I gently set Edin in my arms and slowly, as if wading through quicksand, walk out of the study and up the stairs to her bed chamber. My mind races as I push through her doors and lay her limp body down on the bed. I tuck Edin's hair behind her pointed ears, taking in every small detail of her beautiful face. Placing a cold rag over her forehead, I kiss her cheek, and lay down next to her, waiting for her to wake.

I took her to the veil before she was properly trained. What will I do if Edin does not recover from this? It is a burden I fully intend to bear for all eternity. I will have to be torn away and put to death before I ever leave her side, and even then, I will always return to Edin.

CHAPTER 61

ENDRICKS

The tapping at my window wakes me. A crow is perched outside with a letter attached to its leg. "Right on time," I smirk, opening the glass pane. Since only gods are able to open the veil between realms, I was forced to send a letter back to Helheim with my request regarding Edin's next task. I untie the scroll from the crow's leg. "Thank you," I mutter, giving the bird a piece of bread. "Now go on," I huff, waving it away. Crows are known to be quite nosey. They have been tasked with delivering messages, as they are the only creatures able to travel freely between the realms. I pry open the Helheim wax seal and read over the short letter.

Endricks,

Your request has been granted and will arrive in one day's time through the veil. Do not disappoint me.

King Adonis

I smile, "Excellent." Tossing the letter into the fireplace, I begin making preparations for the next training session. After witnessing Edin harness her power in the Deadwoods, I am sure with the right motivation she will finally be able to tap into it and control her magic.

CHAPTER 62

EDIN

"Good morning, my Little Hellion," I hear Osiris say as he brushes my hair behind my ear. I crack open my eyes, and he kisses my forehead.

"Oh my gods," I mumble. My body feels as if it was in the War of Realms. "What happened?" I groan, curling up to Osiris.

"When you touched the veil, it seemed as if your body had not quite become accustomed to that amount of power yet."

"Ugh!" I groan again, burying my face in his chest.

"All in good time, Edin. Do not fret, I know you will get the hang of it," he says, stroking my hair and kissing the back of my head. "You are the Goddess of Purgatory, Edin."

I look up at him and run my fingers through his red wavy hair. "Thank you for always being so supportive," I say, tilting my head up for a kiss.

His lips meet mine, "Of course. I am just glad you are okay. Now, you stay here in bed while I go make breakfast." He slides out from under me, piling pillows all around.

"Thank you," I giggle.

Osiris slips on his cotton pants but leaves his shirt on the back of the chair. I run my eyes up his toned tan body, landing on his handsome face as he pulls his hair back into a low knot. "Stay put. You need to rest your body," he smiles, giving me a wink.

I slowly sit up in bed, adjusting the piled-up pillows under my sore limbs. Looking down at my hand, I notice the faded purple marks that climb up my arm. I trace over the electrical lines with my fingers as my mind goes back to last night. The amount of power I felt coursing through my body when I touched the veil made it seem as if my heart might give out. I pull *Death's Grimoire* from my bedside table, finally taking a moment to look at it. The book sends a faint spark of electricity through my hand as I flip open the leather-bound cover. I read over a list of names and each individual's role in life, their death, and then their judgment.

- **Name:** Geneva Parsynth. **Life:** Village water sprite. **Death:** Smoke inhalation while assisting in town fire. **Judgment:** Elysia.

- **Name:** *Calveran Bartosh.* **Life:** *Village prophet never caught for spreading false information.* **Death:** *Natural causes.* **Judgment:** *Helheim.*

"You really do always get what is deserved in the end," I mumble to myself. Before I can continue reading, the list of names disappears, and a new set of names takes its place. Flipping through the pages of the new list, I notice there are not as many names and all of them have an undecided judgment next to them. I assume the previous list belonged to Cato and now this is my list of fates to decide.

The sound of the bedroom door opening startles me. I jump, slamming the book shut. "Hello again, my beautiful Hellion," Osiris greets me with a smile. Butterflies build in my stomach, as I watch him walk in shirtless with a delicious-looking tray of food. "I apologize for taking so long. I was not sure if you prefer a sweet or savory breakfast," He says, setting the tray down on my lap.

"You did not have to do all this," I say in shock, looking over the mountain of food and the single tulip in a vase.

He kisses my forehead, "I know. I wanted to."

CHAPTER 63

OSIRIS

Edin scoots over in the bed patting the now empty area, "Join me?" she smiles.

"How could I say no to such an offer with that smile?" I slide into bed, grabbing a strawberry, and popping it into my mouth. Edin goes for the toasted bread, smearing fig jam across it, while I opt for a pork roll.

"Now that you have had some time to adjust, how do you feel about your new life in Purgatory?" I ask her. She takes a moment to answer, washing her food down with a sip of tea.

"Purgatory definitely takes time to get used to, but oddly, I find it very beautiful and calming here. The grey and gloom reminds me of the bedtime stories my mother used to tell me."

I toss a sausage to Nyx. "And it is all yours now," I say, watching the hound catch the food mid-air.

"As soon as I am able to open the veil I plan to bring my mother to visit. She will adore you!"

I smile, "I would be honored."

"Oh! And Blythe!" Edin squeals, almost choking on her tea, "Gods! She will have a fit finding out what we have been up to!" She giggles giving me a wink. I can not help but laugh with her. Her face turns somber and her laughter fades, "I miss Blythe dearly. Back in Windemere, we were inseparable."

I wrap my arm around her as she pulls her knees up to her chest. "You are almost there, my Little Hellion. I know as soon as you are able to open the veil I will be seeing fox ears coming through."

"By the way, why do you call me that?"

"My Little Hellion?"

"Yes," she nods, "You know I am a Nephilim, only half hellion."

I poke at her horns, "Because of these cute little horns and your absolute viciousness." I playfully bite at her. The same smile as before appears back on her face, bringing a sparkle to her eyes.

She takes my hand, intertwining her fingers with me, "I am quite fond of you, Osiris."

"I am quite fond of you as well, Edin," I respond, kissing her. The same shock that I have grown comfortable with runs through me as our lips meet.

She giggles, "You know, Endricks is going to explode when he hears about the veil incident."

"Undoubtedly so," I chuckle.

"It can be our little secret," she giggles, giving me another kiss.

A banging at the castle door echoes throughout the halls, loud enough to reach Edin's bed chambers on the second floor. "Speak of the hellion," I joke, raising an eyebrow at Edin.

She quickly finishes her toast and pulls my tunic on. I follow behind her, watching Edin and Nyx walk side by side down the stairs and through the great hall to the castle doors.

CHAPTER 64

ENDRICKS

Edin swings open the castle door. "What a lovely way for you to greet us this morning, Endricks," she smirks.

"Training leathers," I respond flatly, not allowing her to get under my skin this early in the morning.

She huffs, stomping off while mumbling, "Fucking insufferable." She is gone before I am able to hear the rest of her sentence, but I can make a guess and it brings a smile to my face. My eyes wander back to Osiris, feeling his stare on me.

"Osiris," I nod.

"Endricks," he grimaces, "Please come in and have a seat while you wait for Edin."

I step inside, choosing to take a seat in the great hall. I roll my eyes as Nyx bares his teeth at me. Osiris sits down in a chair across from me, questioning, "What do you have in store for training today?"

"It does not pertain to you."

Osiris throws his hands up, "Just attempting to have a conversation." Thankfully, our chat is cut short as Nyx runs up the stairs meeting Edin on her way down.

"Ready," she grunts, slipping a dagger into her thigh holster.

I watch Osiris kiss her. He grabs her face, whispering, "You got this, Little Hellion."

Rolling my eyes, I give them my back, yelling over my shoulder, "Courtyard."

She is not a damsel.

CHAPTER 65

EDIN

I give Osiris one last kiss before he leaves for his duties in Elysia. Calling Nyx to my side I make my way out to the courtyard. "Miss me?" I laugh.

"No," Endricks tilts his head, "Are you ready to begin today's training?"

I roll my eyes, "Yes."

He nods behind me and I spin around. My jaw drops and I rub my eyes, blinking, unsure if I am actually seeing what is before me, *who* is before me. I turn back to Endricks, giving him a puzzled look.

"Is this real?" I ask, pointing back behind me, still in disbelief.

He rubs his temples, "Yes, now go on."

Spinning back, I rub my eyes one last time, still unsure if I believe him before I frantically take off running. A figure descends the steps of Gehenna Castle and a set of fox ears come into full view.

"Blythe!" I scream.

"Edin!" she yells back.

I crash into her, full force, sending us to the ground laughing. Tears stream down both of our faces. "What? Why? How are you here?" I cry.

"I was summoned here."

"Why? Shit, I do not care right now. I missed you so much!" I cry, hugging her. I pull her up off the ground.

Blythe waves her hand up and down my body, "Look at you, Miss Goddess! In these tight-ass leathers, you look hot!" I roll my eyes at her. "What happened after the Enlightenment? We all just received a letter that you were sent for training for your new title, no details," she asks me.

"Well," I scratch my head, "The two men you saw me dancing with..."

"Yes?"

"The winter wine may have gone to my head," I laugh.

"And?"

"And I may have had a threesome with them, passed out, and woke up here," I say, throwing my arms up.

Blythe squeals, "Oh my gods! It was about time."

"Anyways, welcome to Purgatory," Nyx sits down at my feet, "This is Nyx, my familiar."

"He is," she cautiously pets him, "Cute."

"I will introduce you to Osiris later."

Blythe smiles, "The fine-ass General from the Enlightenment? He is still here with you?"

"He is," I giggle.

"Who is the hot broody man over there?" Blythe points behind me.

I roll my eyes, "That would be Endricks, the man placed in charge of torturing, I mean, training me."

Blythe and I make our way over to Endricks. "Endricks, this is Blythe," I say.

"I am well aware," he sarcastically responds, "I am the one who requested her arrival with the approval of my father, King Adonis." Blythe sticks out her hand to Endricks, he respectively takes her hand with a bow.

"That was awfully kind of you," I raise my eyebrows at him.

He runs his fingers through his coal-black hair, "Yes, kind."

"I am going to show Blythe around Purgatory," I grab her hand and we begin to walk away.

"We have training, Your Highness," Endricks sternly states.

I yell over my shoulder, "I am well aware. Blythe just arrived, give us an hour." I continue pulling Blythe towards the castle, my mind races with all the things I need to tell her about. "I have so much to show you!" I squeal, my excitement overwhelming me.

I feel a tug pull me back and the weight of Blythe's arm suddenly becomes heavy in my hand. "Blythe?" I spin around. The look of shock runs across her face. "Blythe!" My eyes scan down to her chest, and my stomach drops as bile rises in my throat. I scream, my vision blurring at what I am witnessing. A shard of ice protrudes from her sternum. "Blythe! Oh, my gods!" I scream, catching her as she falls to her knees, coughing up blood. "No, no, no!" I jerk my head up, "Endricks! What the fuck?"

He slowly steps over to us, "This is your training, Edin."

"What in all of Helheim is fucking wrong with you?" I yell.

"Back in the Deadwoods you were able to compel Nyx's soul back into his body, you need to channel the same energy."

***

I wildly tear Blythe's sleeve, holding the cloth against her chest, trying to contain the bleeding. "You asshole! I already told you, I have no idea how I did that!"

"But you can. Feel for your magic, Edin. The ice is melting and it will only become more and more difficult to bring her back."

Tears stream down my face as I look back down, screaming, "Blythe, listen to me, please stay with me!" I try to calm my breathing and focus on my magic, but I can not hear anything over my pounding heartbeat. I look back up to Endricks. "Help me," I demand.

He squats down, "I can not help you with this part. You know what to do."

I can feel the ice shard melting under my palms, as I continue to hold pressure. I begin taking deep breaths trying to stop my shaking hands. *You can do this, Edin. You are the Goddess of Purgatory.* Forcing my breathing to slow, I look inward for my magic. The familiar erratic shock of my power courses through my veins.

"Blythe, listen, you can not die. You are not welcome in Purgatory yet," I cry. I reach out, searching for Blythe's soul tether, almost like back in the Liminal. *Shit! I can not feel anything!* "Endricks! What am I even looking for? There has to be more to this than just commanding her back into her body!" I growl.

"Think of all the things that remind you of Blythe. What color her soul would be. How she makes you feel."

I close my eyes and begin searching for all things reminiscent of Blythe. My mind begins to shift, and I feel like I am falling. I crack open my eyes to a foggy white mist that seems to go on for an eternity. "Blythe!" I scream, spinning my head around. I spot the soft glow of a green light off in the distance. The feeling of comfort envelopes me, reassuring me that I am heading in the right direction. I take off sprinting, continuing to sift through all things Blythe in my head. *The beautiful flowers that she conjures. Her laugh, and our silly banter. Our friendship, and how she is always there for me.* The glowing green light comes into view, and vines begin to form. The scent of jasmine spreads around me, and flowers bloom. *Blythe's favorite flower.*

The braided cord of a green and gold tether is finally visible and I feel the warmth of our connection pull on me. The air around me thumps in rhythm with her faint pulse. "Blythe!" I stumble, landing on my knees. Scrambling to get back up, the tether seems further away than before, and fear seeps into my bones. "No, no, no! Shit!" My hands begin to shake again, as the panic of losing Blythe takes over. My heart pounds and sweat forms across my forehead, as I am suddenly being dragged away from her soul cord. I search for anything to grab onto,

watching Blythe's soul fade in the distance.

CHAPTER 66

ENDRICKS

I watch Edin fall back off of Blythe's body, gasping. The purple mist encircling them begins to dissipate.

"No!" she yells, "I was there, Endricks. I could see her tether! What…what happened?" She looks around, "How is the sun already setting? It was just midday."

"You were searching for Blythe's tether for hours. Time no longer exists after death."

She looks over at Blythe, the ice shard gone, and the puddle of blood that surrounds her. "It was happening so quickly, it felt like minutes. I have to try again Endricks," she sobs.

"I will carry Blythe inside and you may try again in the morning. You have exhausted your magic."

"In the morning? I can not leave Blythe like this until the morning!" she growls.

I reach to pick up Blythe's body, "Edin just let me-"

Cutting me off, she smacks my hand away, yelling "Do not touch her, you bastard!"

Nyx snaps at me. I take a deep breath, trying not to lose my composure "You have seventy-two hours from the time a being passes to properly compel their soul back into their body. Now if you would just let me help!"

"No," she yells, "You have done enough! Just leave!"

"Edin."

"Fucking leave," she sobs.

Nyx lunges at my hand again, barely missing me.

I huff, "Fine."

I start to turn away as I watch Edin fall across Blythe's body holding her. Taking another deep breath, I head back to the guest quarter. With every step, I remind myself that this is for the greater good.

This is the push Edin needs.

CHAPTER 67

EDIN

I lie on Blythe's chest, tears streaming down my face as the sun sets. Nyx nudges my hand, whining, trying to console my shattered heart. Nyx continues until I pull myself up off of Blythe. I wipe my swollen eyes, looking down at her pale body. Brushing the hair from her face I whisper, "I will bring you back, Blythe."

I lay my hands back on her chest, shut my eyes, and blow out a slow deep breath. Focusing on my heartbeat, I feel inward for my magic once again. The same erratic shock runs through me, but it is faint. I slip back into the white mist searching for the green glow of Blythe's tether. My mind races through memories of us.

Her smile, how it could light up an entire room.
Can. *How it* can *light up an entire room. Her*
protectiveness over me.

The smell of jasmine sweeps through the air. I turn
in the direction of the scent and I catch a glimpse of a
green glow. I take off running. *The way she takes my hand*
in hers when she notices I am anxious. Blythe's cord
comes into view, vines twist all around blooming jasmine
in front of me. I push through the vines, my arms becoming
heavy and my steps suddenly sluggish.

"What is happening," I cry out. It takes all my
strength to lift my boot for the next step. I fall to my knees.
"Blythe," I scream, "You are not welcome here in
Purgatory! You must return to Windemere!"

The green and gold braided cord is just out of my reach and I begin to drag myself. I try to lift my arm, reaching for her tether, but they feel like dead weight. "No, please, no," I sob, watching the vines wrap around Blythe's cord as the green glow starts to fade.

"Shit!" I scream, opening my eyes to Purgatory. I slam my hands down on the ground, crying, snot dripping down from my nose. Nyx sits down next to me, leaning his warm body against mine. He nudges his head under my arm, trying to help me stand.

"Thank you," I say, rubbing his head as I get to my feet. "Endricks said I had seventy-two hours to bring Blythe back," I huff, "Well, forty-eight now." Looking down at Blythe's body, her lips a deep blue, my tears begin anew. "I need to get her inside," I mutter, lifting Blythe's head.

Nyx slides his head under her body, allowing me to lift Blythe onto his back. We make our way back inside Gehenna Castle and the feeling of defeat crawls over me, causing my chest to ache. Slamming the doors shut behind me, I yell, "Sera! Get a fire started in the library!"

Sera comes running down the great hall, tripping over her feet when her eyes land on Blythe. "Dear Gods, almighty!" she shrieks.

I watch Sera's gaze run from Blythe's body to my blood-smeared hands, wanting to question me, but she takes off toward the library.

"Come on, Nyx," I command, slapping my hand against my thigh as we follow Sera.

CHAPTER 68

EDIN

I begin lighting candles, scouring the library, searching for anything that will save Blythe. I huff, tossing a book down. Every book I come across has a similar scripture, "Only a necromancer can compel a soul back into a being's body. The act of commanding a being back into one's body is an emotionally daunting task, aligning one's soul with another."

Sera comes running back in with a stack of blankets.

"Shit!" I yell, throwing another book onto the floor. I lean against the bookcase, taking a breath, trying to calm my nerves. *Anger is not going to save Blythe.* I look over the library, the room in disarray, dozens of books now strewn across the floor. I watch Sera cover Blythe, who already lays in front of a roaring fire, with another blanket, as per my request.

"Miss Edin," she whispers.

"Yes," I growl.

"I am not sure if these blankets can help her."

I rub my temples, "I know, but it is the only thing I can do right now. I have searched this entire library for any book that might help me."

Suddenly a thought comes to mind. *Death's Grimoire. There must be some sort of scripture that can lend me some guidance.* I leave Sera where she sits, taking off in a sprint upstairs. Rushing into my bedroom I notice the fresh vase of tulips by my bed, and after grabbing the book, I dart back out.

No time for distractions, Edin.

I crash back through the library doors, startling Sera. Grabbing a candle, I hold it above the book as I flip through the pages. *Blank. Blank. All fucking blank.* I stare down at the back cover, only the first several pages are filled with undecided judgments of souls.

"Fuck!" I yell, slamming *Death's Grimoire* onto the floor. The book lands on its spine, opening to the sixth page half full of names. I begin to walk away as something catches my eye. Dropping to my knees I look over the page where there looks to be a smudge. I squint, trying to read the almost illegible script. Breaking into a cold sweat I crawl back, away from the book. The room around me begins to blur as my heart beats wildly in my chest. "No," I beg. "No, no, no! I still have time."

Reaching for the book again with shaky hands, I run my finger over the name. The text is blurry and faint, but Blythe's name is now written in *Death's Grimoire*. I clench my jaw, dragging my nails across the floorboards. All I can hear is my heart pounding in my chest as my sadness turns to rage. "This is all fucking Endricks' fault," I hiss, picking myself up off the floor. I swipe up another book, swinging it against the wall. "He knew I was not ready! I told him I had no idea how I saved Nyx!" I turn to Sera, who is still shaking with fear that streaks her face. "Sera, stay here with Blythe, keep her warm."

"Of course," she stutters out.

Slamming the door shut behind me so hard the stained glass windows rattle, I head to the guest quarters.

CHAPTER 69

ENDRICKS

I sit on the edge of the bed, leaning over, running my fingers through my hair. I could hear Edin on her rampage all the way from the castle door. My door crashes open, sending the handle through the wall. "Oh? We no longer knock?" I grumble, turning to look at Edin stomping in.

"How fucking dare you!" Edin screams, her face a shade of red and her knuckles white from how hard she seems to be clenching her fist. "You knew I was not ready, Endricks!"

"Edin, this is the last task you need to complete for your training. If you can compel a soul, you can open the veil," I say, standing from the bed.

"Why not another rabbit," she yells, "Why Blythe? My best friend!"

"Because you needed to be emotionally attached to this soul," I say, walking towards her.

She laughs, shoving me, "And what would you know about emotions? You are a heartless tyrant, just like King Adonis."

The comment strikes a nerve, making my eye twitch. "Edin," I growl.

"No! Do not *Edin* me," she growls right back, shoving me harder as she begins to cry. "You have never cared for another soul in your life. How dare you put me in this position!"

My vision begins to turn black around the edges, "You do not know anything about me," I snarl.

"From what I have heard, it sounds like you are following right in your father's footsteps!" Edin yells, shoving me against the wall. I grab her by the throat, swing her around, and slam her back against the stone wall.

"I am not my father," I grind out through bared teeth.

"Prove it," she spits, tears streaming down her face.

***

I crush my lips against hers, not allowing another word to leave her vile little mouth. I squeeze her neck, easing my tongue into her mouth. Edin swats and scratches at my hand begging for air, stirring a feral urge within me. My hand stays at her throat, keeping her pressed to the wall, but I pull myself away before things can escalate.

Sheer astonishment creeps up Edin's face, then shifts to rage.

"Endricks," she growls, gasping for air.

She backhands me, sending a pin-pricking pain across my cheek. Edin jerks her fist up preparing to punch me. The familiar warmth of her touch envelops my body. I meet her gaze, watching the flicker of a flame turn into an inferno behind her gold eyes. She violently grabs a handful of my hair, forcing her lips against mine. Returning the kiss, I bite down on her lip, causing her to whimper.

CHAPTER 70

EDIN

My body feels as if it is set alight. The heat that washes over me as we kiss is otherworldly, traveling down between my thighs. I rip open his tunic, pulling back to look over his toned chest and the intricate black tattoos that cover his torso. Endricks grabs me by the face, bringing my gaze back to his, and kisses me again. His other hand slides down, unlacing my leather top, and freeing my breasts. His hand moves further down, snapping the buttons clean off my pants and tearing them down my legs.

Endricks grabs my ass, and I wrap my legs around his waist while he lifts me up. He slides me up the wall, the stone scraping at my back, as he leaves a trail of bites and kisses down the side of my neck and to my chest.

Wrapping my legs even tighter around him, I grind on him, begging for a release.

"So needy," he smirks, biting and licking back up my neck.

I arch my back towards him, absolutely dripping with said need. Endricks coils his fingers into my braid, wrenching my head back. I hear the thud of his belt hitting the floor just before the stretching burn of Endricks' cock pushes into me.

The pain quickly turns to pleasure as he brutally thrusts into me. I moan, taking all of his length. The heat between us is scorching, sweat begins to drip off my chest. I drag my nails up Endricks' back, making him let out a feral growl. Framed pictures crash to the ground, shattering, as he pounds into me. I grab a hold of his black horns, taking control. Slamming myself down on his cock, I lean in biting down on his lip drawing blood. I ferociously ride his dick, jerking his head back with each thrust. My heart pounds, feeling the erratic pulse of my magic run through me. Endricks grips my throat, cutting off my breath. I toss my head back, moaning. I squeeze my eyes shut as he begins pounding into me even harder than before, digging my nails deep into his back. Blood drips down his spine as Endricks yanks my braid even harder, making me arch my back to a straining degree. He thrusts into me, seeming to hit the exact spot that makes me lose control.

I scream out as I am sent over the edge. Purple fireworks explode behind my eyelids as my orgasm crashes over me. The erratic burst of my magic rips through my body, suddenly falling in line with my heartbeat, intensifying my pleasure. Another thump beats with my pulse, and I realize it is his own heartbeat intertwining mine. I begin grinding harder, in rhythm with his thrust, riding out the waves of my orgasm. Endricks throws his head back, moaning as he finishes. I slowly open my eyes, meeting Endricks' gaze.

"Oh gods," I groan, the crushing weight of reality hitting me. My stomach turns as rage and disgust settle back in, not only towards Endricks, but now with myself.

How could I let my emotions get the best of me while Blythe lies dead in my library, and with Endricks of all people? The man who murdered my best friend.

Shoving Endricks off of me, I quickly snatch up my tattered clothes from the floor. I head straight for the door, taking one last glance over my shoulder at the destroyed room. Endricks stands with his back to me, pulling his shirt on when I notice something that sends a chill down my spine.

"It is you," I stutter out in astonishment.

"Come again?" Endricks grunts, turning towards me.

I feel the heat in my face build as my anger skyrockets. My head spins with realization. There, on Endricks' shoulder is a fated mate mark.

"The masked man from The Enlightenment, it was fucking you!" I yell.

"Edin, you do not understand the ramifications of the situation."

"Oh, I understand. You can fuck me, but you do not even have the courage to tell me you are my fucking mate?"

"We can never be together," Endricks growls.

"You took it upon yourself to make that decision?" I grind out.

"I did," he spits.

"Well, you do not have to worry about that. I could never be with a heartless brute like you, fated or not."

CHAPTER 71

ENDRICKS

The pain of her words cut deep even though I know this is how it must be. My hatred for my father soars. I have always been his little puppet, but I will not allow Edin to become one. The thought of my father abusing Edin, forcing her to do his bidding is too overwhelming. I send my fist into the stone wall, yelling, "I am only trying to protect you!"

"Protect me from what, Endricks? How many times must I tell you I am not some damsel in distress?"

I keep my back to Edin, looking over the cracked stone, "You do not know my father. You do not know the hellish cruelties he is willing to inflict to gain power." Memories of my mother sweep through my mind.

"What does your father have to do with this? Is that why you are my trainer?" Edin snaps.

I breathe out, trying to calm my rage, never expecting to explain myself to her. "Over one thousand years ago, when I was held in the Helheim Prison, a prophecy that I would be fated to the next Goddess of Purgatory was revealed. My father saw this as an opportunity to strengthen Helheim, using a Goddess's judgment to cast more beings into Helheim while lowering the numbers in Elysia. As heir to the throne, my father expects me to uphold, if not better, Helheim in this vision.

Edin cuts me off with a huff, "What do I have to do with you and your father's feud?"

"When fated mates become one, they gain immense power and are able to extend their life expectancy. You are a goddess, Edin. You may choose to live for an eternity, and I would as well. What better way to ensure one's reign than with immortality?"

"You knew all of this and you still chose to come to Purgatory?" she barks out.

"Yes, I chose to come myself and make certain that you despise me so much that you would never choose to be with me."

"You succeeded, Endricks. You lied to me, killed my best friend, and then fucked me, only to tell me I am some pawn in King Adonis' grand scheme!"

I swing around, meeting her stare, "Would you rather have had it my father's way? Purgatory be attacked? Gehenna Castle raided? Hellions do not take prisoners, Edin. They slaughter anyone in their way! Do you want to be chained to a throne? Forced to cast judgment as my father sees fit?" I yell.

"I would not fucking allow it!" Edin snarls.

I laugh, "The day I came to Purgatory you could not even wield your magic. How would you have intended to fend off an entire army?"

Edin furrows her brow, not saying a word. "I chose to come here to protect you from my father."

"Why? If you never intended to be with me, then *why*, Endricks?"

"I watched my father tear my mother apart, drain her of her very soul, just to gain power. My mother had found her fated mate, she was in love and happy, but her family also held great power. She was torn from her mate, shortening her life expectancy. She was forced to bear an heir for my father. Me," I say through gritted teeth. "The pregnancy stole any fight she had left in her. Once he had been given an heir, she was of little use to him. My mother was thrown in Helheim Prison. Then, I was placed in the prison, and as additional torture, my cell was adjacent to hers. I was granted the view of watching my mother waste away to a shell of her previous self before she died."

Edin stares blankly at me, confusion clouds her face, "Endricks, I do not understand," she says, taking a step back from me.

I huff, pinching the bridge of my nose, "Gods Edin! It does not matter if we are never allowed to be together, you are my fated mate! My soul was precisely fabricated for yours! I refuse to let harm come to you, including my father's wrath, even if that damns me. I will tear the very seams of these realms apart if you are what lies between them, Edin."

CHAPTER 72

EDIN

I feel the color drain from my face. Taking another step back, I search for the door handle behind me with my hand. "Endricks," I stutter, my mind overwhelmed with emotions.

King Adonis wants to use me as his pawn. Blythe is dead, and only I hold the power to resurrect her. Endricks is my fated mate, he would tear the very realms apart for me. He lied to me, kept me in the dark, and slaughtered Blythe. We can never be. But Osiris...shit. Osiris has cared for me this entire time, no fate needed, and this is how I treat him. I am just as much a monster.

Finally, feeling the handle in my grasp, I swing the door open as quickly as possible. "As soon as I open the veil you will leave and never return. You are no longer welcome in Purgatory, Endricks," I state.

"Understood," he says, giving me his back.

Slamming the door shut, I slowly make my way back through the castle gates. My heart breaks all over again for Blythe, and now Osiris as well.

"How could I do this? And with Endricks?" I huff.

I continue berating myself with every step to the castle. Pushing through the large doors of Gehenna Castle, Nyx greets me, seeming to have stood post here the entire time. I walk back into the library, finding Sera right where I left her. "Thank you, Sera," I say, taking Sera's hand, "You may leave us for the night."

She reassuringly squeezes my hand, "As you wish, Miss Edin."

I watch Sera take her leave before turning towards the fireplace. Blythe lies in front of the fire like a statue, rigor mortis set in. Pressure builds in my throat as a cry escapes my lips. I fall to my knees next to her body, the newfound knowledge too much to bear. Looking over Blythe's beautiful, ashen face, I push her auburn hair off her forehead. I lean down, kiss her cheek, and curl up next to her. "I am so very sorry, Blythe," I whisper. "I will bring you back. I promise."

Tears stream down my face and the pain in my chest intensifies as silence finally falls around me. Nyx lays down against my back, attempting to comfort my broken heart. Unfortunately, my mind opts to do the opposite. I lie holding Blythe's cold body as every moment of today replays in my head like a cruel joke. The joy I felt seeing Blythe for the first time in weeks. The look of shock and pain that clouded her face as she was impaled. The sheer terror that ran through me as I held pressure to her wound, silently begging the Gods to save her, and the irony that I am the Goddess I beg for, yet I have no idea how to wield my power. My anger towards Endricks for his violent actions with Blythe. The warm comfort that enveloped my body when Endricks and I fucked. I could feel our very souls almost intertwine, setting me on fire from the inside out. The way my magic finally hummed in tune with my heartbeat. The feral rage and betrayal sinking in at the realization that he is my fated mate. Then the crash of guilt for Osiris washed over me. Only to return here, to Gehenna Castle, and see my best friend, still dead, with no help from me, taking the final blow. I gasp for air, choking, as the pain in my chest intensifies. I have cried so much that I no longer have any tears left in me. Rubbing my swollen eyes, I curl up next to Blythe, holding her tight.

CHAPTER 73

ENDRICKS

"Fuck!" I yell, throwing another fist through the stone wall. Forcing Edin to hate me was exactly my plan, and now I hate myself for betraying her. I allowed my emotions to get the best of me. "I knew this woman would be my downfall," I grind out, looking over the crumbling stone. I sit down on the bed, slicking my hair back. My mind replays our last moments together and I can almost feel her touch.

The way Edin's body fit so perfectly against mine, her golden eyes set alight, reminded me of a blazing fire, as I pounded into her. The pulsing hum that ran through me as our magic and souls intertwined, felt so right. Then, the look of disgust across her face when she realized that I

am her fated mate. I hurt Edin, but at least now she

understands the dangers of Helheim, of my father, and of

me. Once she is able to open the veil, I will take my leave

and deal with the consequences. Even if I can never truly

have Edin, I find solace in knowing she will be safe.

CHAPTER 74

EDIN

The sun breaks through the stained-glass windows of the library, waking me. I stretch my aching neck, wincing at the pain from sleeping on the floor. My eyes adjust and I am once again hit with reality as I look over at Blythe. Tears brim my eyes and a lump builds in my throat. I swallow it back, fighting off the tears. I refuse to let my emotions get the best of me today. I pick myself up from the floor and head upstairs to shower, knowing I must first help myself if I plan to help Blythe. I push through the door to my bed chamber and walk straight to the lavatory. Quickly stripping out of my blood-stained training leathers, I stand in front of the mirror and look over myself. Dried blood covers both my hands and streaks my face. My hair is a knotted mess. My eyes pan down to my chest, where my goddess mark is ingrained in my skin. Determination pumps through my veins. "Edin, you are the Goddess of Purgatory," I say to myself, still looking in the mirror. I let out a deep breath, as I unbraid my hair and step into the shower. I turn on the hot spray, allowing the water to soothe my aching limbs. Taking my time, I sprinkle a few droplets of clary sage and frankincense around the floor to calm myself, breathing in the steamy aroma. I lather my hair and let it soak, before moving on to washing my body. The water at my feet is tinged pink from my blood-covered hands, making me grimace. I quickly finish rinsing off, no longer wanting to be in the shower. Stepping out and drying off, I wrap myself in a silk black robe. I walk back into my bedroom to find Sera coming in with a tray of food.

"Good morning, Miss Edin," Sera greets, "I was hoping to have this in here for you before you finished. I guess these old bones just don't move as quickly anymore." She smiles at me, trying to lighten my mood.

"Thank you, Sera. I truly appreciate all you have done for me."

Sera sets the tray of food on my bed, "Is there anything else I may fetch you, Miss Edin?"

A thought comes to my mind, and I quickly ask, "When Osiris brought my things, did he happen to bring anything other than clothes and toiletries?"

"Oh, yes ma'am. There were a few chests as well. I placed them on the top shelf of your wardrobe," Sera says, opening the doors.

My heart soars as I snatch a piece of toast and scramble over to Sera. "Perfect," I squeal. "Keep the fire going in the library. I will be down shortly."

Sera hurriedly leaves.

I begin hoisting down the large chest, rummaging through it for exactly what I need in hopes of saving Blythe. "Where in all of Helheim is it?" I grunt, starting to panic, unable to find it. I jerk down the other chest, and it drops to the floor with a thud, spilling all my things. My eyes land on a dried flower crown and I feel like I can breathe again. I carefully pick it up. As soon as Blythe was able to wield her earth magic, she conjured a garden of flowers out of excitement and then made this crown for me. I look over the scattered items on the floor and also find the seashell Blythe gave me the day we met. Now that I have everything I need, I rush to throw on clothes and shove the rest of the toast in my mouth. I head back to the water closet, quickly snatch up my mother's healing salve, and then run out of my room toward the library.

CHAPTER 75

EDIN

Pushing through the stained-glass doors of the library, I look around the room. Everything is back in its place. All the books I had thrown are perfectly organized back on the shelves, as if it never happened. I turn to the fireplace, and the scene before me hits me in the gut all over again, taking my breath away. Squeezing the seashell tight in the palm of my hand to ground myself, I walk over to Blythe's grey body lying on the rug. Candles are set around her with large puddles of wax pooling around them. Blythe lies with her hands placed one on top of another, and a pillow under her head; three blankets covering her body. If it was not for the greying of her skin and blood smears across her face, it would seem as if she was peacefully napping.

"Sera?" I choke out.

"Yes, Miss Edin?"

"Will you bring me a warm basin of water, some towels, and a clean change of clothes for Blythe please?"

Sera nods, making her way out of the library for my requested supplies. I swallow my nerves and kneel down next to Blythe. Nyx joins me at my side with a whimper.

"I will resurrect you, Blythe," I whisper, grasping her hand.

Sera rushes back into the room, sloshing water onto the floor as she sets it down and hands me a stack of towels. "I will return with clothes for Miss Blythe," Sera says, turning back to the door.

I quickly get to work, wiping the dried blood from Blythe's face. Working my way down her neck, I unlace her top. My stomach turns as I look over the gaping hole in her chest from where the ice shard impaled her.

"Fuck you, Endricks," I growl, beginning to clean the edges of her wound. Once clean, I reach for my mother's healing salve. Opening the wooden lid, I take more than necessary and spread it across the edges of Blythe's injury. I look over at Nyx, "It is worth trying. Right boy?" Carefully, but quickly, I change her clothes, attempting to respect her privacy as much as possible. A small chuckle breaks my lips, knowing Blythe would not care if anyone saw her naked. She has always been so comfortable in her own skin.

***

I finish lacing Blythe's clean top and sit back on my feet. Closing my eyes, I take a few deep breaths to calm myself. *You can do this Edin. You are the Goddess of Purgatory.* I reopen my eyes and place the dried flower crown on Blythe's chest and the seashell in the middle of the ring. Leaning forward, I kiss her forehead, whispering, "Come back to me, Blythe."

I place both my hands on the crown, pressing the shell into her sternum with my thumb. Pushing a slow breath out, I close my eyes, feeling for the erratic pulse of my power. My magic comes rushing forward, igniting my body. I feel it creep through my chest and down my arms. The immense pressure swells in my lungs as if I am suffocating. I shove back the nerves and realize it feels just as it did when I was with Endricks. My magic no longer feels unstable, but flows through me, aligning itself with my heartbeat. It sounds off in my head, like the slow beat of a drum, building more power with every thump. I take hold of the newfound feeling as my confidence rises.

Opening my eyes to a white mist, I look down at the flower crown in my hand. The flowers are no longer dry and brittle, but full of life, as if they were freshly cut. The smell of jasmine swirls around me, and I turn my head to the right. The faint glow of green peaks through the mist and I take off in a dead sprint. Clutching the crown tight, I sink myself deep into the memory of the day I received it. Blythe's excited squeals echo all around me as a field of flowers begins to rise through the mist. I can see Blythe with her hands held high, overtaken by her newly gifted power. I can hear my own laugh echoing with hers as we embrace, swinging each other around and falling into the flowers. Whispers of our conversation bounce all around. "This is amazing." "It is beautiful, Blythe." We slowly sit up, our stomachs aching from laughter. Blythe reaches out, plucking a handful of flowers. I watch as she braids them into an intricate crown. Placing the crown on my head, Blythe whispers, "Just like you."

The sound of our giggles fade with the memory, and the glowing green shines brighter. Vines of jasmine start to form, blooming before my eyes. The flower crown is no longer in my grasp, but I feel the small, curved edges of the seashell tight in my palm. I think back even further into my memories of the day we met. It was a cold, hazy winter day in Blackburn. I was out on a delivery, barely old enough to remember all the turns of the cobblestone streets. Looking down at the hand-drawn map my father made for me, I stumble and fall to the ground. The wooden crate of jarred salves cracks open and the jars roll across the street. I hurriedly pull myself up in a panic, snatching up the delivery. I hear a small voice behind me, causing me to jump.

"I'm so sorry."

I turn around to a small set of fox ears and bright green eyes. The girl looks to be around my age, but I have never seen her here in our small village. She hands me a jar of salve.

"No, I am sorry. I was not paying attention to where I was going," I say, taking the jar.

"My name is Blythe," she whispers.

"I am Edin. Are you new here?"

Blythe looks down, "Yes, my family just moved here from the southern border."

I grab her hand and smile, "Welcome to Blackburn."

She looks back up at me with a shy grin and begins helping me pick up the rest of the jars.

"Thank you, Blythe," I say, putting the last of the jars back in the crate, "I live a couple of streets up in the cottage with the stained-glass windows."

She giggles, "We are only a couple of houses down from there."

"Perfect," I giggle back.

Blythe takes my hand, "Thanks," she places a small shell in my hand, "For being so kind in this new place."

She turns and heads in the opposite direction. I look down at the shell, taking in its beautiful reflective colors. I had never seen a shell before, as I had never been to the southern border. From that day forward we were inseparable, spending every moment together. Blythe told me all about the beaches, painting the most gorgeous images in my head. In return, I showed her around Blackburn and all the most beautiful mountain views.

The memory fades just like the last, but the warmth in my chest builds. The jasmine vines now flood my vision, enveloping me in the scent of Blythe. I push through them, following the green light that shines between the leaves until I reach an opening. The gold and green tether of Blythe's soul hangs in the center with vines intertwining down it in braids. The hum of my magic radiates from my fingertips as I reach out for it. Tears of joy stream down my face as I finally am able to grab her lifeline.

"Blythe," I command, "Come back to me!"

The vines pulse with my power, and the smell of jasmine intensifies. All the memories of Blythe rush over me. "You are not welcome in Purgatory, Blythe!" I scream.

"Edin." I faintly hear.

My heart soars at the sound of her voice reverberating throughout the mist. "Come back to me Blythe," I cry out. I focus all my power through the braid, squeezing tight. "Please!" Everything begins to shake around me, as I command Blythe, "Come back to me!"

Falling to my knees, my power feels too much to bear. Squeezing the tether so tight my knuckles turn white, I scream, "Blythe!" The force of my magic sends me onto my back.

"Edin?" I hear behind me. I scramble to my feet, turning around. There before me stands Blythe.

"Blythe?" I choke out, slowly stepping forward, unsure if this is real.

Blythe runs towards me, crashing into me with an embrace. "Edin!"

CHAPTER 76

BLYTHE

As I crash into Edin, feeling her warm embrace, I'm suddenly gasping for air. I rip my eyes open. My vision is blurry, but I'm no longer in the mist. I'm laying on the floor in a library and time seems to move in slow motion. Air painfully spreads through my lungs causing me to cough.

"Blythe," I hear Edin say. The pressure of her embrace calms me as reality speeds back up. Edin lets go of me and places her hands on the sides of my face.

"Oh, Blythe, I thought I lost you forever," she cries.

I reach up, placing my hand over hers. "Never," I hoarsely say.

My vision clears and I can finally see her tear-streaked face. Edin's eyes are bright red and irritated with dark blue circles under them. The look on her face brings me back to my last moments alive. Panicking, I scratch at my chest, trying to unlace my top.

"Blythe. Blythe!" Edin yells, grabbing my shaking hands. "It is okay. You are okay," she says in a calmer tone.

I watch as she unties the laces to my top. I reach to where I last felt the piercing cold pain tear through my chest. It now feels solid and warm, with slightly lifted edges where the shard once was.

"What happened, Edin?" I say, my voice cracking, "We were walking towards the castle, and then this sharp, cold pain ripped through me. I couldn't breathe. I remember you screaming, but I couldn't make out what you were saying. The cold crawled throughout my body, down to my toes, and up my face. Then suddenly everything was warm and it all went dark."

Edin brushes my hair from my face, "Let's get you settled and then I will explain, okay?"

I nod my head in agreement and another woman comes into view.

"It is nice to finally meet you, Miss Blythe," the woman smiles.

"This is Sera, my housemaid. She cared for you until I was able to bring you back," Edin says, looking up at Sera. "And I am forever in your debt for that, Sera. Thank you," she says to Sera.

Sera drops to her knees beside Edin, laying a hand over both of ours. "It was an honor to be of service in such a trying time, Miss Edin. No thanks are needed."

CHAPTER 77

EDIN

Sera and I slowly help Blythe up from the floor.

"Gods, my body is as stiff as the dead," Blythe whines.

Sera snorts at Blythe and I just roll my eyes with a smile at

her typical comment.

We make our way over to the leather sofa with

Blythe's arms hanging over our shoulders. Settling Blythe

down, I grab as many blankets as possible, covering her to

bring her body temperature back up.

"I will go make you a bowl of the stew I've been

simmering all morning, Miss Blythe. It will warm you

right up," Sera chirps, and then turns to me, "Would you

also like a bowl, Miss Edin? You must be hungry."

I look out the window, realizing the sun has started to set. Time truly does not exist after you pass. It felt like I only spent maybe a few hours retrieving Blythe. I nod to Sera with a smile, "Thank you."

Sera returns with a tray in hand, two bowls of steaming stew and crusty bread on it. I sit across from Blythe at the other end of the couch, staring in disbelief. *She is actually here.*

"Thank you," Blythe says, taking a bowl.

"Yes, thank you, Sera," I mumble, still in shock.

"You both are so very welcome. I will leave you two to chat," Sera says, making her way back out of the library.

Blythe slurps her stew slowly, "Edin?"

I jump, startled out of my own thoughts. "Yes?" I smile.

"Are you okay?" she asks. I laugh at her concern, she is the one who was just resurrected from the dead. "Please do not worry about me right now. I am fine," I say, my mind racing.

"Okay," she drags out, not believing a word I am saying, "Then fill me in on what happened."

I look down at my stew, grimacing at the thought of everything that has played out. I rip a piece of bread from the loaf, handing it to Blythe, and then tear my own piece off. "You better get comfortable because you are in for a tale," I laugh.

CHAPTER 78

BLYTHE

I sit with my mouth agape, listening to Edin explain everything that happened from the moment I died. *I still can't believe I died and then was resurrected.*

"Wait, so Endricks brought me here as a lesson for your training?"

Edin nods her head.

I roll my eyes, grumbling, "I thought he was being nice."

She sarcastically laughs at me, "Endricks does not have a nice bone in his entire body, but I also had to learn that the hard way. He always has an alternative agenda."

"And you tried to command me back into my body and failed?"

Edin grumbles, "Twice."

"Then you pretty much rage fucked Endricks."

She huffs, not able to look at me, "Again, unfortunately, yes. I am so sorry, Blythe."

I scoot closer to Edin, grabbing her hand, "Don't be sorry, Edin. I'm sorry that bastard is your fated mate, but it sounds like it was able to help you resurrect me." She gently squeezes my hand.

"I mean, yes. I could feel my magic intertwine with his when we fucked, and ever since, it has felt more in tune with my body. The intensity of my power intertwined with Endricks' is heavy, but now I am able to control it."

I can't help but burst out laughing as the idea that comes to mind, "Well, let's use his own power against him. Open the veil and kick his ass back to Helheim, Edin."

Edin joins in on my outburst, laughing, "You sly fox! I missed you so much. I think that is a perfect idea."

I have to wipe tears off my cheeks from laughing so hard. "So, Blythe, while you were dead, what did you see? Could you hear or see me in the mist?" Edin questions, finishing up her stew.

"It was dark, or maybe I just couldn't see anything, but it was so calm. I heard your voice once in the beginning and I tried to call out to you. Could you hear me?"

"Not at first. The first two times I tried to reach you were silent, but this last time I could hear your laughter all around me."

"Yes! It was as if it started as an echo and built up."

"Exactly! When I was close enough to reach your soul tether, your voice was so close," Edin squeals, happy to know we were experiencing the same thing

"What was that like? My tether?" I excitedly ask, setting my elbows on my thighs while resting my hands on each side of my face.

Edin smiles, "Just as I had imagined, it was beautiful. The brightest gold and emerald braided together to form a cord stretching beneath the mist and as high as I could see. Jasmine vines were blooming everywhere; the smell was intoxicating in the best of ways."

"Thank you for saving me, Edin."

I reach out to her for a hug and Edin meets me halfway, responding, "Never thank me for that, Blythe. You are my best friend."

I release Edin from the embrace, "Now tell me about this angel of a man of yours."

"Oh gods," Edin swoons, as her cheeks turn red, "Osiris."

"Go on," I giggle.

"Where do I even begin? I can not even say he is Elysian sent, because that would be an understatement, even though he is."

I can't help but squeal with excitement, "I have waited so long for this moment!"

We spend the rest of the night talking all about Edin's *adventures* with Osiris, and the veil, and then about Purgatory......*Boring.*

CHAPTER 79

EDIN

The morning sun breaks through the stained-glass windows, waking me. I stretch, realizing Blythe and I fell asleep on the couch. Looking over at a sleeping Blythe, full of color and life, brings tears to my eyes, but I will not allow them to fall. *She is back. She is safe.* I roll off the sofa, wincing at the pain in my neck from sleeping in odd positions to fit on the couch with Blythe. I tiptoe across the room and swing open the library doors, the smell of bacon and coffee wafting in.

Blythe's eyes fly open and she stretches as she sits up. "Do I smell bacon?" Blythe says with a yawn.

"You would be correct," I wink. Blythe has always had a large appetite for her stature.

Nyx perks up from his bed in front of the fireplace. We make our way across the castle, through the dining hall, and to the kitchen. To no one's surprise, there stands Sera in front of the wood-burning stove.

"Good morning, ladies," Sera rings. "It is so nice to see you both up and well. Now go on and have a seat while I finish up here."

Blythe bumps my shoulder, whispering, "Breakfast ready as soon as you wake? Can I just stay here?"

I push her off me, "You were almost a resident of Purgatory, Blythe. No."

She huffs at me, rolling her eyes, "Fine."

Walking back into the dining hall we take our seats, waiting for Sera.

"Come on, Edin. Couldn't you make me, like, a lady of the court or something?" Blythe whines.

I roll my eyes, just as she did, "No, because I am not a queen, or royalty, for that matter."

"You are the goddess of this realm. I am pretty sure you can do whatever you like."

I reach out, grabbing Blythe's hand, "As much as I would love to have you here by my side every day, I know your place is back in Blackburn."

Blythe squeezes my hand, rubbing her thumb across the back side, "Again, fine, but only if–"

Sera cuts off our conversation, coming in with plates stacked up her arms, full of different breakfast dishes. "I wasn't sure what Miss Blythe would enjoy, so I made a little of everything," Sera says, setting plate after plate down.

"Thank you, Sera," I nod.

"Yes, thank you so much," Blythe chimes in, her eyes the size of saucers at the mounds of food before us.

"Any plans for today, Miss Edin?" Sera questions with a smile.

Before I can answer, Blythe jumps in, "We will be heading to the veil today."

I choke on my orange juice, coughing out, "Is that so?"

"It is," Blythe smiles curtly.

Sera pats her hands on her apron, "Well, I think you will be just fine today, Miss Edin. I mean, Blythe stands before us in the flesh, all at the hands of your doing."

407

Blythe smirks across the table at me, "I am so glad you agree, Sera. Could you have the guards on standby to escort Mr. Endricks back to Helheim, please?"

"As long as that is what Miss Edin wishes," Sera says, looking at me.

"Yes," I huff, "Have the guards ready on my orders."

"As you wish," Sera says, taking her leave from the dining hall.

Blythe wastes no time stacking her plate high with food and immediately devouring it. I opt for toast, as my stomach is in knots from thinking about the task at hand today.

"Edin," Blythe scolds from across the table. "Quit biting your lip and get out of your head. I will be right by your side."

As usual, Blythe's words comfort me. "I know, it is just nerves from the last time I was at the veil," I shrug.

"Things are different now," she says, stuffing an entire piece of bacon in her mouth.

"I know," I huff, picking at my toast and sliding Nyx a piece under the table.

CHAPTER 80

BLYTHE

Edin and I finish our breakfast in silence, her nerves obviously getting the best of her. We head back into the kitchen, setting our plates down in the sink, and thank Sera again for the amazing meal.

"I could get used to that," I chirp, trying to at least get a rise out of Edin.

She rolls her eyes, "We have already gone over this, Blythe. Come on, let us get changed and we will head towards the veil."

I begin following Edin back through the dining hall to the castle entryway, where a grand set of stairs sit. We make our way up the stairs, and all the way down the hall. I look over the painted portraits of ancient men and grimace. Edin pushes open a set of doors to a room fit for a queen.

"You say you aren't a queen, yet this is your bedroom," I say, throwing my arm towards the oversized bed.

"It was like this when I got here," Edin laughs, "Calm down." She walks over to her wardrobe, pulls open a drawer, and tosses some clothes at me.

I look down at the training leathers, "Why do I need these?"

"Because I am not sure what all is down in the lower corridors of the castle, and it just feels fitting," Edin shrugs.

I pull the leather top over my head, saying, "At least I will look hot, these things are skin-tight."

"Not the point," Edin grunts, pulling on her own leather pants.

CHAPTER 81

EDIN

We finish dressing and head back out of the bedroom, down the stairs, and towards the back of the castle to the study. I look at Nyx, "Stand guard here for us. Will you, boy?" Nyx seems to understand and sits down at the door to the lower quarters.

Sera walks in as I pull the candlestick from its holder, just as Osiris did before. "Miss Edin, Osiris has returned from Elysia while you both were upstairs readying yourselves. He is in the kitchen having tea," Sera says.

"Have him wait for me in the den, please."

"As you wish," Sera nods, walking back towards the front of the castle.

"You don't want Osiris with us?" Blythe
questions, raising an eyebrow.

I breathe out, torn with my decision, "I do, but I
also do not want, or need, the distraction."

"Understandable. That man is *very* distracting,"
Blythe laughs.

I reach for a torch from the crate and light it with a
flint match. We descend the staircase, and the chill of the
lower quarters sends a shiver down my spine. The dark
hallway illuminates, and rats scurry into the shadows.
"Come on," I nod towards Blythe. I take a deep breath,
attempting to remember the path to the veil. I begin
running my fingers across the walls, feeling for the stone
ridges, just as before. We come to a fork, and my finger
finally catches on a ridge. "This way," I say, taking a right.

We turn the corner, and spiders begin to climb out from the cracks between the stones. *Blythe's fear is spiders.* I stop walking and calmly turn around towards Blythe. "Blythe," I rest my hand on her shoulder, "The lower corridors are enchanted, and they will try to create illusions to keep you out."

She scrunches her face, "Oh, okay," she says, not understanding the point I am trying to get across.

"The enchantment plays on your biggest fears, Blythe."

Her eyes go wide, and she tilts her head, looking past me. "Spiders! Absolutely not!" Blythe screams.

Spiders start to crawl around my feet, encircling Blythe's boots. Blythe jerks her shoulder from my grasp, squirming. Panicking, she starts stomping at the spiders as they climb up her legs.

"Blythe," I yell over her screams of terror, "Blythe!" I watch as she swipes and scratches at her torso, starting to hyperventilate. "Blythe! It is an illusion!"

Blythe rips at her training leathers, crying. The spiders continue to climb her body. Her screams of terror echo throughout the halls, piercing my ears.

"Blythe," I shout, slapping her across the face, unsure of what else to do. The smack brings her out of her panic, and she locks eyes with me. "It is not real, Blythe. This is part of the enchantment; it feeds off your fears."

She stumbles back, and I step forward into her, firmly grabbing her shoulder. Blythe tries to take a breath, wiping her tears. "I promise, they are not real."

"Promise?" Blythe stutters out between breaths.

"I promise." She takes a deep breath, pushing it out slowly.

"They're not real," she says, in a much calmer tone. The spiders begin to fade into shadows, then completely disappear. "Oh, thank the gods," Blythe cries. "What the fuck was that?"

I shrug, "It is part of the enchantment to protect the veil from intruders."

"What the fuck," she grumbles.

"Sorry for slapping you," I smile.

Blythe rubs her cheek, "I kinda deserved it," she snorts. "Come on, let's get this over with."

We continue to take turn after turn down the hallways, following the ridged stones. The cobbled walls shift with every new hall. "It's like a damn labyrinth in here," Blythe huffs.

"We are almost there, I think."

We take a few more turns, and the set of large wood, silver, and sapphire doors come into view. A weight lifts off my chest, "Finally." I lift the latch, and the doors swing open on their rusted hinges with a screech. My heart races with thoughts of the last time I was here. *The pull of the veil. How I wanted so badly to reach out beyond this realm. The pain that rushed through me. Then everything went dark.* I shake the thoughts from my head, peering up at the veil at the other end of the long room. I set the torch in a holder, and step up onto the catwalk, making my way across. Blythe follows close behind me as the torches on the walls begin to rekindle on their own accord.

We reach the other end, just in front of the foot of the second set of stairs. Closing my eyes, I take a moment to ground myself. The pull of the veil seeps into my bones, and I can feel the hum of its power rattling through me. My magic rushes in, pounding in tune with my heartbeat like a drum.

Blythe grabs my hand, giving it a light squeeze and a smile of reassurance. We walk hand in hand up the steps. The veil stands before me, just out of reach. The same purple mist rolls out around us and down the stairs from the swirling vortex of color. Closing my eyes, I focus on my magic and picture the description of Elysia.

I slowly raise my palm to the veil. Sparks begin to reach from the veil, connecting with my hand, and I push forward, making contact. Electricity runs up my arm in varying shades of purple. The electrical shocks nip and bite at my skin, creating streaks of lightning up my forearm.

I grit my teeth from the pain, refusing to be overpowered by the veil's immense magic. Bright lights flash behind my eyes as the shocks crawl up my face, and then seeps back down into my chest. I jerk my head down, feeling as if the skin on my sternum is being ripped open where my goddess mark resides. The searing pain subsides and I feel a shift in my soul as the veil's power intertwines with my own. The electrical current runs back down my arm and into the portal. Sparks fly, and the vortex begins to spin faster, turning to a liquid-like state. I stand firm with my feet flat on the ground, forcing my magic out of my palm.

The vision of Elysia runs through my mind on repeat. Suddenly the surface of the veil gives way, but I refuse to stumble forward. The liquid state reaches the corners, the purple fog fading away, and a scene opens up before us.

CHAPTER 82

EDIN

The Golden City of Elysia stands in the frame. I push my hand further in, feeling the warm Elysian sun on my fingertips. Stumbling back, I release a breath that I did not realize I was holding. I blink my eyes in disbelief. Large gold buildings that reach high into the sunset skies with beautiful glass air balloons cloud my view, just like Osiris said.

Joy overtakes me as Blythe squeals, "Edin! You did it!"

I hold out my hand for Blythe to take. She grabs it without a thought, and we place one foot inside the veil, then slowly lean our bodies in. A shiver runs up my spine as we cross and the world shifts around us.

I squint my eyes against the bright light, and the smell of fresh-cut grass invades my senses. A tingling sensation crawls up my back. Looking behind me, I see my other foot still planted firmly in Purgatory.

"Edin," Blythe squeals again, "This is amazing!"

Looking back towards Elysia, I take in the view. Elysians do not keep their veil locked low in their castle quarters, but up high in a tower, overlooking the wondrous city. The gold-arched windows are left wide open, allowing a crisp breeze to flow through the room. From the tower, the view is breathtaking. It seems as if I am able to see the entire land of Elysia from up here.

Blythe pulls me forward, and I jerk her back. "We can not stay," I say, rolling my eyes.

"Come on," she whines.

"We have matters to attend to back in Purgatory."

Blythe wiggles her fox ears, pleading, "Please!"

"We can return later. I promise," I say, pulling her back through the veil. Another shiver runs up my spine as I cross back over into Purgatory.

Blythe shakes her hands, grimacing, "That was amazing, but it feels like the liquid from the portal is crawling all over me."

I rub my arm, looking down to see nothing there. "It is definitely different, but we did just travel to another realm," I shrug.

"Anywho, what's the plan?" Blythe says, as her fox ears perk up.

I half-heartedly laugh, "I will go get Osiris." Heat rushes into my cheeks, and I turn my face to hide it.

Blythe laughs, poking at me, "Someone has it bad for the Elysian man."

"Maybe," I smile.

"I'll go retrieve Mr. Endricks," she says, giving me a sly smile.

I roll my eyes, "Just make sure he gets here in one piece. I do not need all of Helheim on my ass."

"Fine, fine," Blythe huffs, skipping down the stairs and jumping up onto the catwalk.

I follow behind her, quickly making my way across. I lift the torch from the holder and Blythe gives me a pleading look.

"You think I could have a torch, as well?" she says shyly, "You know, with the whole spider thing."

"Here," I giggle, handing her my torch and taking another from the wall.

CHAPTER 83

EDIN

Blythe and I walk back out of the Room of Revelation, leaving the doors open. We begin the journey back down the long, ever-changing hallways. I run my finger across the smooth stone wall and find a ridged stone. "This way," I nod.

Taking turn after turn, Blythe jumps at the sound of the shifting hallway walls.

"Here," I say, grabbing her hand. "The ridged stones will lead you out of the lower quarter. I figured you would feel more comfortable also knowing the way."

Blythe smiles, "Thanks, Edin."

I follow behind her, watching her run her fingertips across the stones.

"This way," Blythe squeals. We make the turn and the light from the study shines down the steps. Blythe takes off running, "Thank the gods, we made it!"

A sound from behind me catches my attention, and I turn around. Standing as still as possible, I listen.

"Come on, Edin," Blythe shouts from the top of the stairs to the study. I twist back around, assuming it must have been a rat. A breeze sweeps through the hall, taking the flame of my torch with it. I pick up my pace. The stone walls begin to shift in front of me, and I take off sprinting.

"Edin!" Blythe yells, running back down the stairs.

The stones slide shut in front of me, leaving me in the dark.

CHAPTER 84

BLYTHE

I slam into the stone wall, "Edin, can you hear me?"

"Yes," I hear her faintly yell through the stones.

"Now, what? Do you think the walls will shift soon?"

"I am unsure. Just go get Endricks. I am sure the walls will have shifted by then," Edin shouts. "Meet me back at the veil."

"I'm not leaving you down here! Have you lost your damn mind?"

"Blythe, we do not know when they will shift back. Just go, I am fine," Edin yells.

I ball my hands into fists, and roll my eyes with a huff, mumbling, "The most hard-headed Nephilim in all the realms."

"What?" Edin calls out.

Not the time, Blythe. Kick her ass later. Breathing in deep, I push out my frustration, or maybe it's the fear of Edin being left alone down there. Either way, I press my palms to the stone, "Be careful, please."

"Always," I hear Edin say.

I push my nerves aside, trying to focus on the task at hand and head back up the stairs. Stepping back into the study, I see Nyx still standing guard at the door. I smile, happy to know Edin has such a loyal familiar. He looks at me, and then down the stairs. "She's okay, boy," I say, cautiously reaching down and petting his leathery skin. "I'll be back soon."

I make my way out of the study and down the long hallway to the entry doors. As I walk past the den doors, I hear a faint conversation between Osiris and Sera, but I can't quite make out what they are saying. My fox instincts pull me towards the door, but I resist eavesdropping. I slip out the castle doors, quietly shutting the door behind me, and head straight for the guest quarters.

CHAPTER 85

EDIN

"Shit!" I yell, slamming my fists into the wall. Panic begins to set in as I turn my back to the stone and slide down it. I could not let Blythe know I did not have a plan. Not after all the shit she has gone through since arriving here in Purgatory. I rest my elbows on my knees, pressing my palms into my eyes, trying to focus.

The walls are constantly shifting, but how often do each of them actually move? I never paid attention to that. Think, Edin! I huff, pressing harder into my eyes. *Osiris said there were multiple ways down to the lower corridors of the castle.*

The sound of a child giggling jolts me from my epiphany. *No. No, no, no.* I jump to my feet, squinting down the dark hallway. Another giggle echoes through the hall, and the hair on the back of my neck prickles. *A fucking carrow.* My heart pounds as the events of my previous encounter with a carrow race through my mind. The fear from my first encounter with the monstrosity flashes through my mind. Its soulless hollow eyes stare at me, and the rotting smell of flesh invades my nose, making me grimace.

A lump builds in my throat as the second encounter rushes forward and Nyx's lifeless body lies before me. Suddenly, I slam back to reality as I feel the hot breath of the beast on the side of my face. Screaming, I reach for the dagger at my thigh and swing in the carrow's direction. My blade connects with nothing, spinning me around. "Focus, Edin," I mumble to myself, laying my forehead against the cold stone wall. *It is the enchantment of the halls. Nothing but an illusion. Carrows live out in the Deadwoods.* I turn back around, trying to regain my composure. I push a slow breath out. Giggles echo all around me, increasing in volume. "None of this is real," I state. The child-like giggles turn darker, sounding more like a growl. The ground begins to shake as if something is coming towards me. The sound of claws scraping along stones grows louder. Dust falls down from the ceiling into my eyes. The floor feels as if it could give out at any moment. I slam my eyes shut and brace myself, shouting, "None of this is real!" Suddenly everything comes to a halt, and an eerie silence falls around me. I rub my temples, "Gods! This fucking enchantment."

I take a moment to calm my nerves, then start feeling around in the dark. I find a wall and begin running my fingers across the stones, silently praying to the gods that I can find my way out of here. I stumble over random left-behind torches, almost smacking my face into the hard wall. *This is the fucking worst.* My heart skips, as my finger thankfully connects with a ridge, and I can breathe again. With newfound confidence, I begin following the randomly placed ridged stones in hopes of another way out. Every turn makes the task increasingly more difficult as I have to reach out to find every connecting wall and feel for the stones.

I make turn after turn and the floor starts to slope upward at a staggering rate. I make another left, and my heart soars when I see the slightest bit of sunlight from around the corner. "Thank the Gods," I huff, running towards the light. I take another turn, and trip over a ladder, landing on my knees. "Shit," I growl, rubbing my shin. I feel the torn threads of my leather pants and blood smears across my hand. Looking up, I see the light coming from up above on the ceiling.

The light shines down around a large stone. I scramble to pick myself up, wincing at the sharp, shooting pain in my knee. Grabbing the ladder, I lean it against the wall and climb up. The brittle wood of the ladder creaks with every step, daring to snap under my weight. I reach the top, and the ladder begins to shake from the pressure. Steadying myself, I press up on the stone, but it does not budge. I shove harder and the stone moves, but only slightly, sending dust and dirt down between the cracks and onto my face. My eyes sting and I breathe in the plume, causing me to cough. The ladder wobbles beneath my feet from the sudden movement, and I hold on for dear life. My eyes burn and I try to hold back another fit of coughs. I spit what dirt I can out of my mouth and reach

back up to the stone. Bracing myself, I close my eyes and

shove as hard as I can.

CHAPTER 86

ENDRICKS

A loud banging at my door shakes the walls. I roll my eyes, assuming it is Edin back to scold me again. I swing open the door with a smile, but it quickly falls from my face. "Edin did it," I say, raising an eyebrow.

"She sure as shit did," Blythe snaps. "Hello, again, Mr. Endricks."

I keep my expression flat, not allowing her to read my emotions. Internally, I knew Edin would be able to resurrect Blythe, and from her arrival I assume Edin has opened the veil. I am quite proud of how quickly she has honed her magic. "And to what do I owe this honor," I say, swinging my hand out.

Blythe smirks and vines begin to grow up through the cracks of the floorboards. They quickly twist around my boots. I reach for the dagger at my side, but my arm will not budge. "No sir," Blythe laughs. She scrunches her nose at me, and her fox ears twitch mischievously. Vines crawl around my hands, intertwining from my left to right arm, and pulling them back behind me. They continue up from my boots, and around my knees, squeezing tightly until I lose my balance, hitting the ground with a thud.

"None of this is necessary," I growl.

Blythe squats down, tilting her head to meet my eyes. "You impaled me with an ice shard," she snarls.

I shrug, the best I can, "Minor details. I take it Edin has successfully opened the veil?"

She pokes me in the nose, "Such a smart Hellion, aren't you?"

I can not help, but smile, knowing I could shred her dainty little vines in mere seconds, if I truly wanted to.

"I'm here to escort your pathetic ass back to Helheim," Blythe spits, crossing her arms.

"Do not threaten me with a good time," I chuckle. The vines wrap tighter up my shoulders, lacing around my torso until I am gasping for air. Blythe squats back down, grabs my chin, and jerks my face towards her own.

"Listen here and listen closely. You will never *consort* with Edin again."

Her words remind me of my father's, and I pull my head back out of her grasp. "Agreed," I growl.

The vines slowly untwist from around my body. I swiftly get up, stretch my neck, and brush the dirt off my arms. I allowed Blythe to have her moment, and I would not hurt another hair on her head for Edin's sake, but my patience is dwindling.

"Perfect. Now that we have an understanding, let's go," Blythe snaps with a smirk.

"Lead the way," I say, lifting my arm towards Gehenna Castle.

She curtly turns, and her fox tail whips around her. I follow Blythe up the stairs towards the castle and through the gates. We walk through the castle doors, passing the den. The halls are eerily quiet. Pushing open the study doors, Blythe and I are greeted by Sera. Nyx turns in my direction, snarling. I roll my eyes, unamused with him.

"Hello, Miss Blythe," Sera chirps. Her smile falls when she looks at me. "Lord Endricks," she nods.

CHAPTER 87

EDIN

Light cascades down onto my face as more dust falls around me. I refuse to stop. After a few more minutes of pounding on it, I am able to slide the stone over. Relief runs through me, taking a weight off my chest. I grip the edges of the opening and painstakingly pull myself up. Panting, I plop my body down onto the stone floor. "Thank the gods," I say, between breaths. I look up at the familiar ceiling with shelves lined all the way to the top, and the smell of lavender floats through the room. *The alchemy tower.* My hand runs across something sharp on the floor, causing me to hiss. I bring my hand up to my face and blood drips down my fingertips. "What the fuck," I mumble, sitting up.

I look over the room. The left side of the shelves and countertop are in complete disarray. Glass jars are shattered and discarded across the floor. Dirt covers most of the countertop. The top shelf that housed the most poisonous plants is empty. I stare at the mess in front of me.

What in all of Helheim happened up here? Who was up here? And why? Shit! Blythe! I run out of the tower and head to get Osiris. *This mess can wait.*

I quickly make my way down the wrought iron spiral staircase, almost missing the last step. I regain my balance, gather my composure, and head towards the den. Pushing through the large wooden doors, I smile at Osiris.

"Hello, Little Hellion," Osiris says, taking another sip of his tea, "Sera tells me you have been on quite an adventure."

I rub my hand against my arm, trying to contain my excitement. Rushing over, I grab Osiris's hand, sloshing his tea, "Let me show you," I wink.

Sera giggles to herself at the sight of us and picks up the tea tray. I pull Osiris out of his seat and back through the den doors. We rush down the long hallway to the study. Nyx greets me at the door. I reach down and rub his head, "Thank you for guarding the door, Nyx. We will be back up soon." Nyx whines, but sits back down.

Assuming Endricks gave Blythe little trouble and they are also on their way to the veil, I pull the candlestick and the door to the lower quarters slides open. Osiris grabs a torch in one hand, my hand in his other, and leads me down the stone steps. Our torch light shines down onto the landing, and I am thankful to see the walls have shifted. We reach the bottom, and I instinctually begin running my fingers across the smooth stone walls. Finding the ridged stone, I tug on Osiris's hand. "This way," I smile. Osiris chuckles, "As you wish," and follows behind me.

CHAPTER 88

ENDRICKS

I nod to Sera and head towards the opening to the lower quarters of the castle. I grab a torch from the crate inside the opening, lighting the tip with the snap of my fingers.

Blythe scrunches her face at me, "You have fire magic too?"

I shrug and begin whistling as I walk down the steps. I hear her growl from over my shoulder.

I take the last step as Blythe catches up to me, asking, "How can a being have both fire and ice magic?"

I feel her eyes burrowing into the back of my head as she follows me down the halls. "How can a being that I just met already be on my very last nerve?"

"I can't wait to watch Edin kick your ass back to Helheim," Blythe smirks.

"Neither can I," I smile. I run my hand along the stone, feeling a ridged edge. "This way," I nod.

"I know," Blythe snaps, rushing ahead of me. Blythe begins running her hand across the stone and takes a right.

I follow her, hearing a faint voice behind me. Ignoring the voice, I turn down the hall. The sound of stones sliding as the walls shift echoes down the hallways. The voice gets louder over the noise, and I can make out my name being called out. The sound of my name stuns me, but I continue walking. We take another right and then a left down the ever-changing halls and the voice grows higher in pitch, whaling my name. Pressure begins to build in my chest.

"Here," Blythe yells, as she takes another turn in a sprint.

My eye twitches as the sound of my name is cried out, directly into my ear. I walk up to the grand doors of the Room of Revelation. As I step over the threshold the cries disappear. The pressure in my chest dissipates and I crack my neck. I take a breath, knowing it was just the illusions of the labyrinth and not the begging cries of my mother calling out my name on her deathbed.

CHAPTER 89

EDIN

We take turn after turn as the walls shift behind us.

The stones begin to close off the hallway in front of us, and

I pick up my pace. I rush to slide through the opening,

pulling Osiris behind me. I cock my head at the sound of

metal bending, and then snapping. Coming to a dead stop, I

whip around in fear of what I may see. Osiris stands

holding his broken sword. "Oh, thank the gods," I breath

out. "I thought it was you that had been smashed."

Osiris laughs, grabbing my chin, "You will not get

rid of me that easily, Little Hellion." I roll my eyes at him,

and turn back around, feeling for another ridged stone.

Taking two more left turns, the flickering flames of torch

light filter out from the Room of Revelation. The sound of

Blythe and Endricks bickering echoes out into the hallway, and my heart soars knowing Blythe is okay. Osiris gently squeezes my hand. I squeeze his hand back and smile at him. He returns the smile with a wink.

We slowly walk hand in hand to the entrance of the Room of Revelation. Anticipation builds in my gut as we stand at the doorway. Osiris clears his throat, cutting Blythe off mid-argument. She swings around, and her eyes grow wide at the sight of me. "Edin!" Blythe squeals. "You made it!" She runs across the catwalk and grabs my face, "You scared the shit out of me. Don't ever leave me like that again!"

I laugh, placing my hand over hers, "I make no promises."

"Seriously, Edin," Blythe grunts.

Osiris clears his throat again, pulling us from our moment and Blythe releases her hands from my face. "Blythe, this is Osiris," I say, laying my hand on his chest.

"Forgive me, I do not think we were ever properly introduced," Osiris says, taking Blythe's hand. "General Osiris of the Elysian Army."

"Blythe of Windemere," she giggles back.

Osiris leans down, and kisses the back of her hand, "It is an honor to finally meet you, Blythe. Edin has told me such wonderful stories about you. I look forward to hearing more from you."

Blythe turns her head towards me, mouthing, "What a gentleman."

A loud huff comes from across the catwalk, "Sorry to interrupt such a touching moment, but, today, ladies," Endricks shouts, rolling his eyes.

"Come on," I say, walking past Osiris and Blythe, and stepping up onto the catwalk.

***

As I walk across I take a moment to look at all the banners hanging in honor of the magic arcane. I never fully took in the beauty of the room before from nerves or excitement crowding my vision. Déjá vu rushes through my head as memories of the Enlightenment come to mind. I felt as though my nerves would eat me alive that night as I walked the halls of Swindon Castle, paying my respects to each of the gods. I had such a closed mind, assuming I would receive healing powers. The fear that ran through me when I received my true power left me in shock. My entire world had been flipped on its head. Now I walk with real confidence through my own castle to the veil, so sure of myself.

WHAT LIES BETWEEN

I am the Goddess of Purgatory.

CHAPTER 90

EDIN

I step off the other side of the catwalk in front of Endricks. The air around us changes, as warmth envelopes me, soothing my soul. He turns his head in my direction at the same time I do, clearly feeling the magnetic pull between us. I push my feelings aside, unable to come to terms with his actions. "Endricks," I curtly say.

"Belladonna," he responds, with a smile.

Osiris steps in between us, cutting Endricks off from my line of sight. Blythe steps down from the catwalk, taking the spot at my side. "Endricks," Osiris growls.

"Ah, General Osiris," Endricks smirks, clasping his hands together. "Always a pleasure to see you."

I roll my eyes, pushing past Osiris. "Enough," I grumble. I take the first step up the stairs towards the veil, and my stomach drops, knowing exactly what I must do. I made the decision weeks ago that I am the master of my own fate. I take the next step, and the tug of my mate's connection with Endricks pulls on my heartstrings. I clench my jaw, reaching the third.

My heart resides with Osirus, fated mate or not. It is a secret I intend to keep for an eternity.

Stepping up onto the platform, the veil comes to life, swirling with electrical tendrils which reach out towards me. Osiris and Endricks come up the steps and stand before the veil. Blythe watches from the catwalk landing. Osiris kisses my forehead and then steps to the side of the veil.

I turn, taking a deep breath. "Lord Endricks, as much as I appreciate your training, as Goddess of this realm I ban you from ever returning to Purgatory for your actions against Blythe," I say, through gritted teeth.

Endricks' eye twitches, but he quickly hides it, adjusting his stance. "Understood," he flatly responds.

I look towards the veil, envisioning Helheim based on the books I have read and old stories my mother spoke about. An ever-burning city of death with a suffocating smog comes to my mind.

Bringing my hand up to the portal, tendrils extend out with a shock, wrapping around my fingers. I wince at the pain as the electricity crawls up my arm. My magic awakens, humming in tune with my heartbeat as it pulses through my limbs. The shades of purple swirl in the veil and spin into a blur. I push my hand forward, making contact. Searing pain radiates across my goddess mark as the full power of the veil once again intertwines with my soul. A tingling sensation starts in my chest, traveling up my head, then back down over my arms and into the portal. I squint my eyes as the blur of purple grows brighter. Finally, the surface gives, turning to a liquid state, allowing my hand to push through.

As the liquid crawls up toward the corners of the frame, the glow of the veil dims. The image begins to shift, leaving me in shock. A massive city of pointed obsidian skyscrapers intricately lined in gold comes into view. Sitting above all the buildings stands a hauntingly beautiful castle made of the same stone and golden inlay. Bridges cross over rivers of fire, and the horizon is filled with smoke.

I take a step back, unsure if this is truly Helheim. The eloquent architecture does not look like it belongs in any of the stories I have come to know about the hellish place. It is both terrifying and alluring.

"Welcome to Helheim," Endricks smirks.

I am at a loss for words. *This is nothing like what I have ever been told, or even read, about Helheim.* "

Finally," Osiris growls.

CHAPTER 91

EDIN

White hot pain rips across my chest, sending me to my knees. I crash to the stone floor, gasping for air. The room begins to spin around me, and a high-pitched ringing whines in my ears. Panic sets in and it feels as if my throat is closing. The pain intensifies, crawling up my neck and I scratch at my leather-bound top, unsure of what is happening. It feels as if I am drowning. The leather gives way, and I tear it from my chest. I stare down in shock at what I am seeing. Running my hand across my sternum, I feel nothing but my smooth skin. I frantically search for the cause of this immense pain. A shrill scream comes from Blythe and the sound of gurgling halts my panic. I jerk my body around, and the blood drains from my face. Time seems to move in slow motion as my brain comprehends what I see.

Endricks is slumped over holding his chest, blood pours from his mouth. A dagger is lodged deep through his sternum, and Osiris holds the hilt. I frantically drag myself backward from the nightmare playing out before my eyes. Osiris jerks Endricks head back, and his lips have already turned a pale shade of grey from asphyxiation. Blue streaks crawl out from the dagger, up Endricks' neck and across his face. The same blue-colored liquid drips off the hilt of the blade. I realize I have seen this blue liquid before and my mind races to connect hidden dots.

The alchemy tower. Nightshade!

"Endricks!" I choke out. I scramble to get to my feet, and another shock of pain rips through my chest as Osiris twists the dagger.

WHAT LIES BETWEEN

The sound of bones crunching echoes throughout the room as Osiris wrenches it from Endricks' sternum. I land on all fours, wildly gasping for air. Endricks hits the ground with a thud.

"Endricks," I cry out, as I pull myself across the floor. I reach out, attempting to grab his hand. Blood spurts from his mouth as his wheezes, struggling to breathe. I feel his heartbeat falling out of rhythm with my own and it seems much fainter. Our fingertips brush just as Osiris hauls his body up into the air. He pulls Endricks blue streaked face up to his own.

"I have waited a great deal of time for this," Osiris smirks.

My body will no longer move, and my vision begins to blur around the edges. I can feel Endricks' heartbeat barely pulsing throughout my own veins. Tears stream down my face as I helplessly watch Osiris toss Endricks' body through the veil back to Helheim.

My gut wrenches, as I cry out, "No!" The purple swirls cloud the corner of the frame. "No, please!" I beg, snot running down my face. The image of Endricks' limp body and Helheim fades away into the purple mist, and the veil seals shut, cutting off my connection to Endricks completely.

My stomach drops as Osiris swiftly turns on his heel in my direction. I attempt to turn my head in search of Blythe. I desperately will my body to move even an inch, but my efforts are fruitless. I can no longer sense Endricks' heartbeat with my own, and it feels as though a piece of my soul has been torn from my body. Osiris squats down in front of me.

"Fuck you," I spit. He grabs my chin, jerking my face toward him.

"It is just you and I now, *Little Hellion,*" he smirks. "I have a few loose ends to tie up first, though." He slams my head back down onto the stone, and pain echoes through my skull, taking my breath, leaving me in a daze. Osiris places a finger on my forehead and growls, "Dispel." The world around me begins to fade, and I am consumed by darkness.

HONORABLE MENTIONS:

THANK YOU TO OUR EDITOR, MARLA VINCENT. WORDS CAN NOT EXPRESS OUR APPRECIATION FOR YOUR KNOWLEDGE AND PATIENCE WHEN WE DID NOT KNOW HOW TO USE A COMMA.

THANK YOU TO OUR BETA-READERS WHO TOOK THE TIME OUT OF THEIR BUSY SCHEDULES TO READ OUR FANTASY SMUT...YOU DIRTY LITTLE FREAKS, MWAH!

STAY TUNED FOR BOOK 2:
WHAT LIES BEYOND

FOLLOW ALONG FOR WHAT LIES
BETWEEN AND BOOK-RELATED
CONTENT ON TIKTOK:
@ROTTINGANDREADING

T.D. FINDLEY HAS ALWAYS HAD AN AFFINITY FOR THE MACABRE, FROM BOOKS TO PODCASTS AND DOCUMENTARIES SHE IS ALWAYS LOOKING FOR THE NEXT BONE CHILLING STORY TO PEAK HER INTEREST. SHE LIVES IN THE NORTH GEORGIA MOUNTAINS WITH HER HUSBAND, THREE GIRLS, TWO DOGS AND TWO CATS. WHEN NOT WRITING SHE FUELS HER SOUL WITH STRONG COFFEE, SNARKY HUMOR AND TRUE CRIME STORIES. ALTHOUGH HER INTEREST IS MAINLY IN INVESTIGATIVE FICTION AND NON-FICTION SHE ALSO LOVES TO DELVE INTO THE WIDE WORLD OF FANTASY AND DARK ROMANCE.

C.N. PETTIT IS A BABY BAT TO THE WRITING WORLD BUT IS A LONG-TIME CONNOISSEUR OF THE SMUT READING COMMUNITY. SHE SPENDS HER FREE TIME REVIEWING NOVELS ON HER TIKTOK PLATFORM, ROTTING&READING. SHE IS A LOVER OF ALL SMUT, BUT THE MORE UNHINGED THE BETTER. WHEN SHE DOES NOT HAVE HER NOSE IN A BOOK OR WRITING HER NEXT NOVEL, YOU CAN FIND HER NERDING OUT, PLAYING CALL OF DUTY, WATCHING SERIAL KILLER DOCUMENTARIES, AND SPENDING TIME WITH HER DAUGHTER. SHE ASPIRES TO ENGULF HER READERS IN THE MOST FANTASTICAL REALMS WHILE KEEPING THEM ON THEIR TOES WITH THEIR THIGHS CLENCHED.